ALI AND HIS RU

Ali and His Russian Mother

BY ALEXANDRA CHREITEH
TRANSLATED FROM THE ARABIC BY
MICHELLE HARTMAN

Interlink Books

An Imprint of Interlink Publishing Group, Inc.
Northampton, Massachusetts

First published in 2015 by

Interlink Books
An imprint of
Interlink Publishing Group, Inc.
46 Crosby Street
Northampton, Massachusetts 01060
www.interlinkbooks.com

Library of Congress Cataloging-in-Publication Data
Shuraytih, Aliksandra.
['Ali wa-ummuhu al-Rusiyah. English]
Ali and his Russian mother / by Alexandra Chreiteh ; translated from the Arabic by Michelle Hartman.
    pages cm
ISBN 978-1-56656-092-4
I. Hartman, Michelle, translator. II. Title.
PJ7962.H74A4513 2015
892.7'37--dc23
                                    2015014302

Cover photo by Hiltrud Schulz

Printed and bound in the United States of America

ALI AND HIS RUSSIAN MOTHER

The 2006 war in Lebanon began on July 12th and lasted until September 8th of that year. Israel's airstrikes devastated much of the country's infrastructure, targeting especially the South of the country and Beirut's southern suburbs, including roads and bridges. The July War displaced over a million Lebanese—a quarter of the population—leaving nearly 1,200 people dead and 4,400 wounded, mainly civilians. For many young Lebanese, it was their first experience of a large-scale war, echoing their families' experiences during the fifteen-year civil war that ended in 1990.

It was in the summer of 2006, on the twelfth of July. We'd just heard on the news that Hezbollah had kidnapped two Israeli soldiers on the border, but this didn't stop us from going out to get sushi. The very second we finished our food, Israel declared war on Lebanon, and everyone working in the restaurant hurried to close up. They asked us to leave right away. So we left right away. Without even paying the bill.

We were lucky. We'd been at one of the most expensive restaurants in downtown Beirut. We'd gone there even though we knew that things weren't normal that day. The streets were practically empty. The restaurant, which usually was packed, was also practically empty, except for us—me, my friend Amal and her fiancé Salim, and two guys we didn't know, sitting at the table next to ours and smoking.

One of the guys at that table looked over at me a few times while we were having lunch. I'd noticed that he'd been paying attention to me from the moment I walked in, and so I made sure to avoid his gaze because his brazenness embarrassed me. But my ignoring him didn't prevent him from being bold and impulsive. Right when we were leaving, he walked up to me smiling and called me by name.

. . .

I thought this was pretty strange. But even stranger, he started talking to me in Russian—it's my second mother tongue, because my mother is Russian.

The guy said his name was Ali Kamaleddin. And then he asked me if I remembered him. I wasn't sure what to answer because I didn't recognize him. He noticed right away that I wasn't sure, and so he explained that we'd been classmates ten years ago, or more, at school in Nabatiyyeh, in the South, where our families were from. He then said that surely my mother knew his mother, because she's Ukrainian. When he mentioned her name, I immediately knew who she was, and then I remembered him, too. I was really surprised because he'd changed a lot from the last time I saw him. And I told him so.

My friend Amal suddenly interrupted our conversation because she was in a hurry to get back to our apartment. Since we'd come out together to the restaurant in her fiancé Salim's car, I had to leave Ali and go back home with them. I said goodbye to him. He answered by turning toward me and kissing my cheek. Then he gave me his phone number and asked me to call him soon.

. . .

In the car, Amal asked me about him—Who's that? What did he want? But her mobile rang, preventing me from answering.

After a few seconds, my phone rang too. It was my dad calling, asking me to come back down to Nabatiyyeh right away because the war had started. I refused, telling him that this "war" was nothing but a bit of disturbance on the border, and it would surely be over quickly, just like always. But he insisted that I had to come back down. When I kept on refusing, he got really angry at me. So I danced around the issue to finish the call without him embarrassing me in front of my friends.

I didn't want to go to Nabatiyyeh, because towns like that suffocate me.

3

Amal's family had also called her, asking her to go back up to Tripoli for the very same reason—the war. My friend protested, saying that she was invited to dinner at her fiancé's family's house, a twenty-minute drive south of Beirut. It wouldn't be logical for her to go to the North right now, because a few hours after arriving she'd just have to turn around and go back in the opposite direction.

After speaking to her family, Amal had completely forgotten about Ali and stopped shooting questions at me. I felt more relaxed then, because I couldn't always take her constant nosiness.

. . .

We'd just finished our phone calls when we got to our place and found our Jordanian friend Sawsan on the verge of tears. She was watching the news on TV sitting next to her boyfriend on the sofa, even though we weren't allowed to have any men in the apartment, according to our elderly landlady's rules.

In the beginning, we didn't pay much attention to Sawsan. We'd gotten used to her getting scared every time the security situation worsened the least bit in any tiny area within the borders of Lebanon. But very quickly we could see that she was much more scared than usual. Amal immediately changed the channel saying, "Enough with your drama!" Sawsan retorted, "What drama? This is war!"

Amal laughed and pointed to the cloudless sky visible through the window, commenting sarcastically, "Then where are the Israeli warplanes?" Sawsan didn't reply. Worry lines multiplied on her face because she'd started imagining those warplanes. A few minutes later, she got even more anxious because our Syrian friend came out of her bedroom, kissed us goodbye in a hurry, and left to go back home to her parents' place in Syria. Sawsan herself left not long afterwards, but just to spend the night at her boyfriend's apartment, because she was afraid of spending the night in our apartment "all by herself."

Amal left to get ready for her dinner, so I stayed at home all by myself. I decided to take this opportunity to call my boyfriend, who lived in Nabatiyyeh, and ask him to come over so we could be alone together at my place. But he said that he couldn't come because the main road to and from the South was blocked for fear that the heavy border clashes between Hezbollah and Israel might reach it.

"Really?" I asked. He answered back, "Don't you have a TV?"

I turned on the television to see what was happening. At that moment I considered calling Ali to ask him if it would be possible to get to Nabatiyyeh before all the roads were blocked, but a breaking news report distracted me.

Israeli warplanes had bombed the main road to the South and destroyed a number of bridges. Secretly, I felt calmer as soon as I saw the blocked road, because it assured me that I would be "stuck" in Beirut. Even if my family wanted to make me come back to Nabatiyyeh by force, they wouldn't be able to!

Then I realized that this was the very same road that Amal would have to take to get back from her dinner party. At that very moment, Amal walked in and said, "You won't believe what's happening!" She told me that she was driving back to Beirut with Salim when she'd heard the roar of a huge explosion just behind them. When I asked her, "Were you afraid?" she replied, "No!" But when I looked in her eyes, I could tell that they were saying the opposite. She went into her bedroom, and I did the same because it had gotten late and I had to get up early to go to the university.

But all classes at the university were cancelld until further notice. That's what Sawsan told me when she came back home the next morning to get some of her stuff before traveling back to Jordan. She was forced to travel on the back roads because Israeli fighter jets had bombed the airport, preventing passenger planes from taking off or landing. Sawsan was really upset because they'd also bombed the road to Masnaa, the border crossing between Lebanon and Syria, in case traffic might be stopped there. They'd been shelling the southern suburbs since midnight.

It took Sawsan only a few minutes to get ready to leave! I walked with her to the entrance of our building, just a few meters away from the main entrance to the university. The narrow road connecting these two entrances was full of students whose faces betrayed visible traces of anxiety. Some of them were talking on their mobile phones. I heard one of them arguing with a taxi driver about the cost of the trip to Syria. Students who had their own cars were gathering up as many of their friends as they could. Sawsan got into her boyfriend's car.

As soon as Sawsan left, I went into the coffee shop next to our building; it was still open because its owner lived in a building nearby. I sat down in front of the window overlooking the street and ordered a lemonade, while looking out at the fleeing students. From time to time, I would hear the sounds of bombs falling on the southern suburbs. I left the café and went into the little shop next door, whose shelves had been completely emptied. I picked up a gallon of water, a box of crackers, and a package of cheese, and walked over to the shop's owner to pay him while looking at the small television in front of him that was broadcasting live images of the destruction from the bombardment. Just then, the picture of a little girl's mutilated corpse flashed across the screen, and I spun around, opened the refrigerator behind me, and took out another package of cheese.

• • •

When I got back home, I threw some clothes and the books I was reading into a little suitcase, and then put on a pair of shoes I'd bought to go running in but hadn't worn in months.

I felt hungry and considered having breakfast. But Amal shouted at me from her bedroom, "They're coming!"

8

By "them" she meant Israeli warships, which were approaching the Beirut coastline that very moment according to all the news broadcasts. I didn't answer. She repeated the information about the approaching warships more insistently, then announced that she'd decided to go back to Tripoli immediately and was taking me with her.

But I didn't want to go with her. I told her this and asked, "Are you hungry?"

She wasn't even able to answer, because at that moment we heard the roar of a nearby explosion that shook the walls of the room. She smiled and said, "We'll be out of here in just a bit!"

We went out onto the balcony to see where the missile had landed and saw smoke rising up from the old lighthouse that was right near our building.

We stayed out on the balcony until my friend's fiancé called and said he was already on his way over to pick her up and drive her to Tripoli. Though his house was only a few minutes away from ours, it took Amal more than a half an hour to choose what she was going to wear! When she finally settled down and we were about to leave the house, my father called to check on me. He'd heard on the TV news about the lighthouse being shelled. I told him I was fine and going to Tripoli because staying in Beirut had gotten dangerous. He got angry and yelled at me, threatening, "You'd better not go anywhere!"

His shouting made me hang on up on him. He called back right away but I didn't answer, and I left home with no hesitation whatsoever.

• • •

When we got to Tripoli, we went up to Amal's parents' apartment on Moawed Street. Her family welcomed me warmly, and her father asked me where I was from. I answered back, "It depends!"

But then to clarify, I told him that my mother was from Moscow and my father from Nabatiyyeh. He answered that in Lebanon we follow the father's line, not the mother's, following up jokingly, "Unless, of course, you're Jewish!…"

I blushed and stuttered but didn't answer. My friend's father noticed that I'd gotten uncomfortable and laughed. The maid walked in and announced that lunch was ready.

I was hoping it would be, because I was hungry, since I'd left Beirut without eating breakfast.

After we had lunch, we went to a nearby pool where we spent the afternoon. We did the same thing on all of the six days I spent in Tripoli. During this time, Amal's parents treated me as if I were a daughter. And I was lucky that they liked their daughter so much and cared about her happiness. They cared about my happiness, too. They gave me everything I needed, and I felt really comfortable around them—much more so than I usually did at my father's house.

My parents called every day to check up on me. It was actually my mother who called, because my father hadn't wanted to talk to me since I'd hung up on him. My mother wanted to come to Tripoli on the back roads through the mountains and bring me back to Nabatiyyeh. But my father refused to go with her. After five days, my mother called me in the morning and told me that she'd threatened my father that she'd go without him if he kept on refusing. So then he had no choice but to do what she asked and get ready to go.

Luckily for me, their plan quickly changed, because Israeli warplanes bombed a convoy of civilian vehicles on the back road leading to the South, killing everyone in it. This news shook the whole country up and paralyzed civilian movement on the roads. My father decided that they'd stay in Nabatiyyeh that day. I relaxed again when my mother notified me of their decision. I told her that I didn't understand why she was so insistent on me going back there! If she really feared for my life, then she should ask me to stay where I was, because the real danger was in Nabatiyyeh, in the South, not in Tripoli, in the North. Besides, life in Nabatiyyeh was unbearable. My boyfriend assured me of this during our daily phone conversations. The electricity was still cut off because the power plants were bombed on the first day of the war. Generators could only be used for two hours a day because of the fuel crisis in the South. This forced everyone to stay awake at night by candlelight. Here, there were no such problems.

My mother surprised me, though, when she said that she wanted to leave the country as part of the evacuation that the Russian embassy was organizing for its nationals. But she wouldn't leave unless I went with her. I told her to go alone if she wanted to go, because I was staying in Tripoli.

Events the next day compelled me to change my mind. The lighthouse just a few meters from the swimming pool where we'd been spending the day as usual was bombed, and then another missile fell on a nearby neighborhood.

In the evening, Amal went to the wedding of a neighbor who lived in the same building. I'd wanted to go with her, but then I decided that I preferred to go to bed early. After a few hours, a loud explosion woke me up, and I jumped out of bed terrified because I thought that Israel had started bombing. I dragged Amal's sister, who was sleeping in the room with me, out of her bed, slid her down onto the floor, and started crawling to her parents' room to warn them of the danger. But she stopped me and explained that people celebrating the wedding had set off fireworks from the roof of the building. She told me to go back to bed and let everyone else in the house sleep.

That was the moment I decided to leave the country.

The final evacuation of Russian nationals was the day after next, so that meant I had to get back to Nabatiyyeh in time to go with my mother to the embassy headquarters in Beirut the following day. I called and asked her to come pick me up in Tripoli.

• • •

My parents left Nabatiyyeh at seven in the morning and arrived in Tripoli around noon. When they walked into the house, I was afraid that my father would start reprimanding me in front of my friend and her family like he always did in front of my friends. But he didn't. I noticed that my mother was wearing running shoes exactly like the ones I was wearing.

While my parents were drinking coffee with Amal's parents, I went to the bathroom three times. The road to Nabatiyyeh is long, and I might not find a place along the way where I could take care of this. For years, I've suffered from inflammation when I hold in my urine, and this makes me feel like I always have to go to the bathroom. When I go, I feel burning, but I don't feel pain unless I've held in my pee. When I don't take care of my need to urinate right away, I cry from pain when I finally do it.

Of course, I've tried to take care of this problem. There's no doctor I haven't seen, no medicine I haven't tried. But it's all been in vain, since whenever my inflammation dies down a bit, it flares right up again. It never goes away.

As circumstances would have it, my inflammation was very strong that summer. This meant that I had to follow the doctors' advice—take anti-inflammatories and drink a lot of water. This, of course, made me have to go to the bathroom even more.

For this reason, I didn't fear bombs on the road from Tripoli to Nabatiyyeh as much as I feared the possibility that I wouldn't find anywhere to pee, since most of the restaurants, gas stations, and shops on the road were closed. But I didn't feel the need to urinate until after we'd left the main road where it was blocked and started up the mountains to reach the back roads. There, we saw a woman sitting on the side of the road selling peaches. We bought some fruit and then asked her about a place where I could take care of my needs. She said that she could stand in front of me and hold up a sheet to block the view from the road. I immediately agreed because I was afraid of postponing something as necessary as this. My mother joined me and urinated behind the sheet, as well. She said that this was a rare opportunity. For a few moments, nothing separated my naked backside from the road and its passersby except a thin sheet. I wondered if Israeli radar could detect us.

After we relaxed a bit and went back to the car, I informed my mother that I had met Ali Kamaleddine, my old school friend who I hadn't seen for more than ten years. I told her that his mother was "Russian" (she is Ukranian, but this is what most people coming from the former Soviet republics are called, as are the languages of all these countries). To help her remember his mother, I reminded my mother of her name. But she put her nose in the air scornfully and told me that she put as much distance as possible between herself and "that kind of woman."

"What kind?" I asked her. I hadn't seen his mother since we'd lost touch, and I didn't really remember her or know anything about her. But my mother stopped there and just asked me to stay away from Ali because, according to her, he was a "troublemaker." My father asked us to be quiet because he was trying to hear the news on the radio and drive the car at the same time. We did as he asked.

The back road to Nabatiyyeh was really long. We didn't get home until evening. Not long after we arrived, my boyfriend came over to say good-bye, and we sat alone in the living room. He asked me not to go, and to stay with him in Lebanon. I smiled without answering.

My boyfriend, who kept insisting that I stay in Lebanon, then left. Not long afterward, the Kleenex factory on the hill across from our house was shelled and caught fire. This prompted a statement from one of the factory's managers. In a television interview, he said that Nabatiyyeh would perhaps now suffer from a tissue crisis. Once again, I decided that I had indeed made the right decision to leave, since I couldn't live without tissues—seeing as I went to the bathroom more than twenty times a day.

. . .

That night, Hezbollah responded by bombing a settlement in the North of Israel, and a number of people living there were killed. The Israeli reaction came, threatening a ground invasion. Immediately after my father heard this news, he started drinking vodka until my mother took the bottle and threw it in the garbage. The amount he drank was enough to make him climb up into the attic and find the hunting rifle that he hadn't used since he had a full head of hair. Talking to himself, he announced that he was prepared to bear arms to defend the homeland! If Israel was trying to force the Lebanese to abandon their country, leave behind their land, let their homes be occupied—to make Lebanon into another Palestine—he would fight them until his last breath! Then he started searching for the rifle's cartridge but he couldn't find it. He took his Russian passport out of his wallet, threw it on the ground, and declared, "Running away is for cowards. I'm staying put!"

I relaxed when I heard that, because if he had come with us to Moscow he would've made our lives a living hell! Our Filipina maid was also happy because she wouldn't be left alone during the war. She had also prepared herself to defend our house—she'd taken the biggest kitchen knife, sharpened it, and put it next to her bed.

• • •

The following day, we went to Beirut with two other families, in a convoy made up of three cars. Traveling like this was safer than us each of us traveling alone. Each family was in one car with the father driving, a Russian flag raised on its roof to alert the assault planes that the passengers were Russian citizens, so they should avoid bombing us. But I wondered how practical this method was, since lots of our neighbors also put foreign flags on their cars, even though they didn't hold a foreign nationality. This made our flag less believable.

We were afraid that we wouldn't be able to reach Beirut, since our cars only had a little bit of gas. Gas station owners would only sell us a tiny amount. Things got even worse when the engine of one of the cars overheated, forcing us to stop every quarter of an hour to cool it off with the drinking water that we'd brought with us.

. . .

After long hours on the road, we finally arrived at the embassy headquarters on Corniche al-Mazraa Street in Beirut. The crowd that had gathered in front of the entrance to the grounds was huge because it included nationals of most of the countries of the former Soviet Union whose evacuation Russia had taken on. Almost all of them were women and children, because the men had decided to stay in Lebanon—either because they found it difficult to leave the country or because they didn't have another citizenship that would allow them to leave.

After a little while, a friend of my mother's came with her daughters. Unlike all of the other evacuees, they had no suitcases. The mother was wearing a summer dress and straw hat, and the girls were wearing shorts and little, light sweaters with swimsuits underneath. They looked like they were ready to go on holiday, not be evacuated from a war zone. This elicited a comment from my mother who said, "Did you get the wrong address?" But they hadn't gotten it wrong. They'd been spending a week in a luxury cottage in Jezzine and didn't know about the evacuations until this morning, so they rushed to Beirut, afraid that it would go ahead without them. I felt sorry for the girls because they were half-naked, and I loaned them some of the clothes that I'd brought. But they weren't useful because everything was really too small.

The women who'd arrived there before us informed us that the buses for the evacuation were parked behind the embassy and that we were going to have to walk through the grounds after showing our passports so that we could get seats.

The women were afraid that there wouldn't be enough seats for everyone evacuating, and so they were all shoving each other viciously in front of the embassy door. Each of them was dragging a big suitcase behind her and using it to push everyone else around her, trying to get closer to the door in order to be the first one to enter when it opened.

After a while the door opened, but only to let the counselor come out. He stood in front of it and announced that the first people to enter would be those families with small children, irrespective of their nationality.

When he was about to go back into the embassy, two women approached and tried to enter, but the guard blocked their way.

We understood that there was no point in going up to the front ourselves, since we had no small children with us. So we waited on the edge of the crowd, making a space for those with the right to advance to do so. We sat on the edge of the road, with our suitcases next to us. The sun had almost fully risen by this time and practically burned our hatless heads, which we refrained from cooling with the little drinking water that we had left. Wiping the sweat from her forehead, one of the women said, looking around her, "Refugees!"

• • •

We really were refugees! However this adjective applied more to some of us than to others. I had seen, for example, a Russian woman wearing a hijab, surrounded by her children, her husband nervously counting his prayer beads. I understood from what they were saying that they'd come from the South—a bomb had fallen right next to their house, which had been partly destroyed, but they'd escaped.

One of my mother's friends informed us that many of the women had been scared or forced to flee from the areas where they lived and worked, and had taken up shelter in the embassy.

"Poor things!" I said. Her answer was that we needn't feel sorry for them because they're prostitutes.

"Real prostitutes?" I asked her. But I didn't wait for her answer and started looking around me, trying to figure out who they were.

• • •

I'd only seen a prostitute once. One evening when I was walking along the Corniche near the lighthouse, a woman had caught my eye because she was wearing a very short skirt and high heels despite the cold and rainy weather. After a while, a young man she didn't know approached her and started stroking her shoulders. She moved away from him, going down onto the rugged, rocky coastline that was covered in garbage. As soon as she stepped on it, her high heel shoe got stuck in one of the cracks between the rocks, and she pulled on it hard until she got it free. Then she sat down and started contemplating the sea. After a little while longer, a huge

22

rat emerged from a dark corner and pounced on her. She was terrified and went back up to the Corniche where she stood on the edge of the road. She waited for a long time before a car stopped in front of her, and she got into it.

The scene I'd encountered was far more exciting than a scene in a film! I had no doubt that watching the prostitutes at the embassy would be equally exciting, especially since I'd gotten so bored waiting. I was able to tell who they were fairly easily because they were women waiting on their own, wearing high heels, and showing a lot of skin on their chests and legs. They were clustered around the door. I stopped a short distance from them and started observing them. One of them in particular had caught my attention because of the big mole between her breasts. After a while, I understood that she was their leader because she stood in front of them as though she were preparing to give a speech. When she motioned with her hand, they got ready and then shouted loudly, "Russia! Russia!"

They had started a protest. Their demand: that Russians enter their embassy first, before the children of the Soviet states and their mothers. Their protest ended quickly because it had angered some of the "normal" women, who expressed their readiness to confront them directly and right away if they didn't shut up.

Then I noticed one woman standing far away from the protest. Like her friends, she left her giant bosom and legs exposed. But when I stared at her, I saw that she wasn't one of them but rather the mother of two grown children, and indeed also a grandmother because her daughter standing near her was carrying her baby girl. Then I realized that her son was none other than my friend Ali.

• • •

Ali saw me and came over. He hugged and kissed me, then wanted to introduce me to his mother. But I got anxious, because merely the idea of talking to her or standing near her distressed me, especially since my mother would be able to see me. I tried to lead him to a place where we could be alone, far from our mothers.

The area around the embassy was deserted, with the exception of a nearby gas station and an army barracks. They were protected from the bombings because of their proximity to the embassy. We walked over to the barracks and stood on the sidewalk across from them. Then Ali lit a cigarette, hugged me again, and said that he was happy to see me. I told him how surprised I was that he was there with the people fleeing the country, because when we were together in school he regularly asserted that he was prepared to die defending Lebanon, and he always used to absolve himself of any connection to Ukraine.

"I am Lebanese in my blood and soul!" He always used to declare.

How could he take refuge in Ukraine, when circumstances in Lebanon right now at this very moment require its strongest men? But Ali didn't answer my question or even meet my gaze. Instead, he stared straight ahead at one of the bare-chested conscripts in the army barracks.

After a few moments of silence, I asked him, "Where have you been all of these years? How is it that you suddenly disappeared from school and no one heard anything more about you?" He told me that his parents sent him to Germany, where he finished school, then university. All that time he really missed Lebanon, though he was scared to return. Finally he wrapped things up and came to spend his summer vacation here. He put out his cigarette and lit another one. Without me asking him, he added that he was forced to leave Lebanon for a number of reasons, and perhaps he could tell me about them later if it was appropriate.

Then he asked me about university and what I was majoring in. I answered that I was studying acting and directing at LAU. He opened his mouth with contrived astonishment, then said laughing, "Oooh, odd choice!"

Him saying this really shocked me because usually only women use this expression. I was more shocked when he hit his cheek with the palm of his hand and added, "Oh for shame!"

His way of speaking reminded me of my grandmother's neighbor Hajjeh Siham, whose life revolved around cooking, cleaning, and taking care of her husband and grandchildren. She covered her large round body with an abaya on the rare, brief occasion when she left the house, looking like a scouting tent. I addressed Ali as a woman jokingly, "What do you mean, hajjeh?"

That really cracked him up, and I felt myself growing increasingly attracted to him. I thought, I wish he'd stay in Lebanon! I hadn't really stopped thinking about him since we'd met in that restaurant a week ago. I was about to tell him all this, but a call from his mother prevented me. She was phoning to tell him that the embassy doors had opened and that people were starting to go inside.

. . .

She and his sister Maria were among the first to enter, thanks to his sister's young baby. When they entered, the women and children from the Soviet states provoked the anger of the Russian prostitutes, standing in front of the door, who quickly started protesting again. One of them noticed Ali's mother's Ukrainian passport, so she shouted angrily at the top of her voice that Ukrainians were occupying the Russian embassy. Ali's mother told her to shut up because she had for her whole life considered this to be her embassy, from the days of the Soviet Union, when that prostitute was still wearing diapers. She added that despite the Soviet Union's collapse she still considered herself "Russian"!

Ali wasn't able to accompany his mother and sister, since one of the guards told him, "Be a man, let the women and children go in first!" Ali was a man and retreated, standing next to me and lighting a cigarette with trembling hands. I was amazed at his constant chain-smoking. I told him so, and he replied that he'd gotten used to it so long ago that he can't hold out long without a cigarette now.

"I'll die!" He told me.

I told him not to exaggerate and asked him if he'd brought enough cigarettes for the whole journey. He smiled, pointing at the bag he was carrying on his back. He said that it contained nothing but cartons of cigarettes! I couldn't figure out which of his comments were joking and which serious.

• • •

While we were waiting our turn to enter, my need to go to the bathroom started to become critical. But it became truly urgent when we finally crossed the embassy garden. I'd decided to go to the bathroom, even though there were very few seats left on the buses, since I was afraid of being trapped on the bus until we arrived in Syria. My mother went with me. This was the quickest pee I'd done in my whole life. When we got back, we found the embassy totally empty and got scared! But right away Ali walked over to us saying that he'd saved three seats—for us and himself—on one of the buses. I found it strange that he'd decided not to sit on the same bus with his mother and sister. On the bus he chose for us, he sat on the seat next to me. My mother sat in the back of the bus next to a woman she didn't really know. I wondered if Ali was doing this as an expression of his feelings for me, which were mutual. I thanked him for looking out for my mother and me. He smiled and assured me that he wouldn't have let the convoy leave without us.

The embassy employees, however, were not in a hurry to leave. This is how it seemed to us in any case, after we'd sat on the parked bus for hours without anyone explaining why. The whole time, Ali was burning up because he was a smoker, and smoking was forbidden on the buses. He seemed anxious, and his anxiety grew minute by minute. I wondered about this because there was no obvious reason why—the shelling was far away from where we were, and our proximity to the embassy protected us from being attacked. When I asked him what was wrong, he told me that he was afraid that we'd never set off, that the Israelis would change their minds about letting us travel and cross into Syria, that they'd bomb our buses and make us into war martyrs! Then he added that he didn't want to die when he was separated from his family sitting in another bus. He preferred to die—if that is what had to happen—near his mother and his sister!

His powers of exaggeration surprised me. I begged him to calm down a little, but he wasn't very persuaded by my words. He then announced that he wanted to smoke.

After a while, the embassy employees told us that if we wanted to use the bathroom or eat something before we set off, we could go to the nearby gas station. We hurried over there, and our arrival enthused the workers who stood us in line and started organizing our movements as if they were traffic cops. They smiled like children in an amusement park. What made them especially happy was the presence of Ali's mother, because, unlike the other women who caught their eye, she understood Arabic and answered their comments with the expression, "Get the hell away from me!" Ali—who was standing behind her—did not help to get them "the hell away" from her. He was busy with other things, since one of the conscripts had come over to him and asked him for a cigarette. Ali was nervous in the beginning and dropped the packet he was holding. Then he bent over to pick it up, and the edge of his shirt flapped up, exposing part of his back. I glimpsed his bright white skin. I stared at it, but then realized that the conscript had noticed what I was doing, so I got embarrassed and quickly moved away from them.

I decided at that moment to phone my boyfriend but discovered that I didn't have enough units left to make the call. The shop in the gas station had only one recharge card left. There were hardly any cards in shops anymore because of the number of people buying them on account of the war. The shopkeeper took advantage of this and started a public auction, eventually selling it to one of the women at double its actual price.

. . .

In the shop, I ran into Ali's sister Maria who was buying sweets for her daughter, and she insisted that I make my call from her mobile phone. When I started typing in my boyfriend's number, the phone suddenly rang. As soon as Maria saw the number of the caller appear on the screen, she cringed and started shivering as if she suddenly felt cold, though it was the middle of summer. I noticed at that moment that the clothes she was wearing weren't appropriate in temperatures this hot, because they were really autumn clothes. Her top, for example, completely covered her arms and neck. I wondered why.

Maria didn't answer the call, and I didn't ask her why. I went over to speak to Ali where we'd been sitting in the bus. We set off taking the road north of Beirut toward the Lebanese-Syrian border. Without missing a beat, he said to me, "She ran away from her husband!"

At first I thought he was joking, but he was serious. He gave me more details, explaining that his sister was living with her husband and their daughter in Nabatiyyeh in an apartment near their mother's house. Her husband had gone to visit his family in the Beqaa on the first day of the war, as he did every week. But she didn't go with him like usual. Their daughter had been sick, and she had to stay home to look after her. Her husband got stuck in the village. It was said that a Hezbollah leader had a house there, and this then exposed the entire village to continual heavy shelling followed by a ground deployment. It became impossible for people there to leave their homes.

Their mother took advantage of Maria's husband's absence and convinced her to join the evacuation, dragging her daughter along with her, even though Maria's husband had forbidden it. She forged his name on a document she wrote for Maria, permitting her to travel. This was in order to follow the embassy's instructions requiring all married women to present official permission from their husbands to leave the country accompanied by their children, according to their religious obligations, rather than civil legal codes. Husbands had to declare that they wouldn't prevent the embassy from evacuating them, so there wouldn't be trouble with the Lebanese authorities at the border.

Had her mother not insisted on leaving, Maria would never have dared to go against her husband's wishes. She recognized the gravity of what she was doing when she arrived in Beirut. She got scared that he would come at any moment and force her to return obediently to his home, despite knowing that this was impossible.

"He'll kill me!" she started repeating to them, adding, "He'll slaughter me like a chicken and pluck my feathers!" Ali kept reminding her that she didn't have feathers. As for her mother, she answered that if he laid a finger on her daughter, she'd make him regret the very day he was born.

I asked Ali why his mother insisted on Maria leaving. He said that Maria had wanted to divorce her husband for years, but she wasn't brave enough to take this step. Her husband knew this and threatened her with prohibiting her from seeing her daughter, if she managed to get her way. This is how he succeeded in forcing her to stay under his roof, because her daughter was the most important thing in her life. But now the right moment had come to get free of him and at the same time remain with her daughter! It came only after long years of torture.

Then he sighed deeply and added, "She doesn't deserve what's happened to her. Her illness has destroyed her life!"

"What illness?" I asked him, but he didn't answer because the people sitting behind us were sprinkling water on us. They were quick to apologize, explaining that it was holy water and they were blessing the bus with it to protect it from bombs.

• • •

We found out that they were Russian tourists who had come to the region to visit the ancient Orthodox churches, discover the origins of their religion, and establish a closer relationship with God. They also informed us that they had visited Israel before coming to Lebanon. So I asked them how they entered the country if they had the enemy country's stamp in their passports? They replied that they'd asked the Israeli border guards to put the stamp on a separate piece of paper and not in their passports. This is what everyone who travels between the two countries does. This information bothered Ali, who gave me a lecture in Arabic. "How can they talk in front of us about their trip to Israel while Israel is bombing our country at this very moment, killing our children, women, and men?" Then he added, "Backwards people!"

I didn't answer because I was busy thinking about the devoutness of those passengers. This is something really recent in Russia. When we were very young, all we saw in Russia were deserted and destroyed churches. After the collapse of the Soviet Union, the authorities began restoring them. People started suddenly regaining an awareness of religion after having learned in school for more than seventy years that God didn't exist. My mother's sister, for example, has begun fasting and going to church. When I visited Russia last year, I found an icon of the Maronite saint, Mar Charbel, with his name written in Russian, in my grandmother's house. I asked my grandmother what Saint Charbel was doing there, and she said that her sister, my mother's aunt, read about him on the Internet, and he had become her favorite saint. So she'd brought a picture of him to my grandmother when she visited her the year before.

I asked Ali about his mother's family—Had they also become believers, and do they go to church? He said no, adding after a pause that there were religions other than Christianity in Russia.

That reminded me of when I'd seen the muftis of the Russian Republic on national television a while before, on a live broadcast of Eid al-Fitr prayers. I asked Ali if his mother was a Muslim, and he was about to answer when the buses stopped at that moment for reasons that the embassy employees didn't inform us of. They suggested we make use of this opportunity to go to the "bathroom," because they didn't know when we'd stop again. Everyone except Ali got out. This surprised me because Ali had repeated so many times that he was craving a cigarette.

• • •

The place where we stopped seemed like semi-vacant land between two cities. After some effort, we found a place that had thick enough bushes to hold us all and cover us from people looking. This spot was very tight for our large numbers, and it forced us to take care of what we had to do all right next to each other. Immediately I found myself flanked by two women, in the middle of a line of women answering the relentless call of nature. At that moment, I imagined that we were squatting behind plants like snipers in films! I also thought, no doubt our collective urination has fertilized this land which soon will sprout into green grass!

After a bit, Maria came over and asked me if I had paper tissues with me. I gave her some and remembered what Ali had started telling me about her illness. I watched her intently for a little bit, but she didn't seem to have any complaints. I expressed this to Ali when I got back onto the bus, and he told me her whole story.

• • •

Their mother was very free in the way she raised her children and didn't forbid them from doing many things that children are usually forbidden to do—like drinking alcohol, for example, or smoking, or watching movies made for adults. Maria's girlfriends were jealous of her freedom that they wished they could enjoy, too. At fifteen she could go out in Jounieh and come back late. She could even have her guy friends over to her house with her mother's consent.

This freedom landed her in a lot of trouble. Once when she had a crush on one of the boys who was much older than her, she started sleeping with him. All of her classmates in school and their families knew about this. So they forbade their children from being her friend, because in their opinion she was a deviant young woman. This didn't affect her too much at the beginning, though, because she was sure that her boyfriend would marry her, like he promised. She thought that this marriage would return her to her previous role in society. But her boyfriend surprised her by marrying his cousin and moving to one of the Gulf countries.

That was a hard slap in the face for Maria! Not long after this, she totally collapsed. So her mother decided to send her to her grandmother's house in Ukraine to start a new life there.

When she finished school, she decided not to return to Lebanon and to complete her university education there, as her mother wished. But then she'd started living with her future husband, who was studying in Ukraine on a scholarship from one of the Lebanese political parties. After they both graduated, he asked her to marry him, and she accepted despite her mother's opposition. She'd decided on marrying young because she'd discovered that she had a serious type of diabetes and needed to get pregnant quickly before carrying a child would threaten her life. She went back to Lebanon with him to live there for good, and they had an official, religious wedding to please his conservative family. The wedding was big, and no alcohol was served except on one table reserved especially for the Russian guests. Then they moved into his family's house in Baalbak where her husband turned into a different person. He forced her to wear the hijab against her wishes and forbade her from working or leaving the house. After her daughter was born, he forbade the daughter from visiting her Russian grandmother.

"Why did he forbid her from visiting her Russian grandmother?" I asked him. He answered, "Because in his opinion, she was a prostitute!"

She was a prostitute, in his opinion, because she went to mixed swimming pools and wore a bathing suit. And because after her husband died of cancer, she married a man ten years younger than herself. He didn't want his daughter to be influenced by her grandmother's deviant behavior. But he quickly was forced to relent a little, since he lost his job and wasn't able to support his family. His mother-in-law scrambled to provide work for Maria in a clothing shop that she managed. She also rented them a house in Nabatiyyeh and bought them a car on a payment plan. Maria's husband then was living off of two women who were supporting him. In exchange, he allowed his daughter to see her grandmother once a week.

• • •

Ali said all of this in English in a very quiet voice, fearing that someone on the bus would hear him. This forced him to get close to me so I'd be able to hear him, and I reckoned this was a good opportunity to express my feelings for him. I stuck my arm to his on the armrest between the two seats and leaned toward him. But he paid no attention and remained sitting there without moving, completely cool and collected. It was like sitting next to a mountain the wind couldn't move! I tried to be more obvious, so I got closer to him and leaned my body against his, when a plane passed over us, letting out a load roar. Ali thought that I was afraid, and so I covered myself with him! He told me reassuringly that he was afraid, too.

But the airplane had really frightened the little girl sitting in the back of the bus, who burst into tears. She didn't stop sobbing for such a long time that I felt my ears would go numb. Ali tried to rescue me from this torture and gave me his digital music player that he'd brought with him, but the only thing it had on it was Fairouz songs.

I remembered how much Ali loved Fairouz when we were in school and how he used to analyze each stage of his life by summing it up with one of her songs. At first it was "Zahrat al-Madaen," "Flower Among Cities." This song brought him to tears, because in that period he used to dream that he'd become a real freedom fighter for Palestine and that he would die so that his homeland, Lebanon, could live! This remained his dream for a long time. Then in the end he changed his mind, saying that he didn't have the ability to kill and that it was better for his homeland if he struggled for it with his mind.

After this stage, he started caring about activism, establishing associations to protest against Israel and organizing meetings and clubs in school. He participated in every demonstration against the enemy, every protest march supporting the Palestinian cause and Arab unity. He used to distribute leaflets that he had written to our classmates on subjects like "democracy" and "the abolition of sectarianism." After the second Palestinian Intifada in 2000, he started to boycott American products and companies supporting Israel. He soon after decided to give up everything he had, including electronics that were made in America.

Then suddenly he entered another nationalist phase and began listening to the song "I Love You Lebanon" all the time. He started considering anyone who hesitated to rank Lebanon as the most beautiful country in the world to be a brute, even though he himself had never even visited any of its tourist attractions.

When I mentioned that to Ali, he said enthusiastically that visiting tourist attractions was all he did during this short trip to Lebanon. He first went to see the towering columns of Baalbak, then tasted the delicious wines of the Beqaa Valley and sat on the banks of the Assi River where he was so enchanted by its bubbling waters that he forgot his worries. Then he visited the sanctuary of cedar trees, the eternal symbol of Lebanon. There he profoundly felt the civilization of this country that had existed for thousands of years. It flowed into him and ran through his veins like electricity! He felt a huge responsibility weighing on his shoulders—the responsibility to complete this civilizational journey—but he didn't know how. When he visited the village of Bcharreh, Kahlil Gibran's birthplace, his desire to be a writer who created masterpieces of world literature increased. He wanted to elevate his country's name, exactly as Gibran did. Ali felt a sort of affinity with him because, like him, he was also an emigrant.

It was in this way that he decided to start writing a novel. He spent a full week searching for a subject for it. But not finding it, he decided in the end to postpone writing until later and finish his touristic journey. He visited Beit al-Din, Deir al-Qamar, and the caves at Jeita. Then he descended from the cool mountains to the hot coastline and swam in the water of the Mediterranean Sea, everywhere from Tripoli in the North to Sur in the South. The journey concluded in Beirut where he savored the tastes of the city that doesn't sleep after having been away from it for many years. He felt thankful for the life burning in it that made him feel alive. These were feelings that he hadn't experienced in a long time.

Indeed, he felt he'd been reborn!

Then his eyes welled up with tears, and he said that he suffers when he sees Lebanon, this beautiful, magical country, destroyed time after time, again and again.

"It's a shame!" he finally said and sighed.

Then he was silent for a while and added that he hoped he would be able to return to Lebanon for good, because life in Beirut was so much better than life in Germany. Germans are crushed by work, and their nerves pay the price. They have no time for human relationships or friendships, and for this reason he always feels cold when he's with them—a psychological coldness that practically gnaws at his bones and permeates his insides even on warm summer days. And his insides are always boiling with his hot Mediterranean blood! But Beirut is warm, alive, and easy. People there are good-hearted, and life there doesn't require too much work.

"So why don't you return to Lebanon then?" I asked him, adding that the war would be over soon and things would go back to normal, as it always does. Or was something else preventing him from doing this?

"So many things!" came his reply. When I asked him to clarify, he said, "My homosexuality!"

He said this as though he were stating something obvious, like the fact that the earth orbits the sun. But this news totally shocked me, and Ali was surprised by my shock because he thought that I'd known that he was gay for a long time.

"Since the last time you visited me at my house!" he said directly and precisely, and I immediately knew what incident he was referring to.

. . .

We were about fifteen years old at the time, and we always went to his house after school because no one was there in the afternoons. His mother was a widow who worked straight through the day until evening, and his sister lived in Ukraine with her grandmother. His brother went to a boarding school in Beirut that specialized in helping people with special needs, before eventually moving to his grandmother's house in Ukraine. Ali's house was an escape from my house—my parents were always home.

We used to spend most of our time watching American films and sometimes watched films that had daring sex scenes. It must have influenced us in some way, because one day we decided to discover sex together. We went into his bedroom and locked the door with a key, even though it wasn't necessary. Then we took off our clothes, but nothing happened because Ali wasn't ready. This really embarrassed him—he locked himself in the bathroom and didn't come out until after I'd left to go home. He didn't invite me to come over anymore.

He told me that even back then he was gay but hadn't known it yet. He'd discovered his homosexuality thanks to what had happened between us. He added that I was the only girl he had loved before realizing that he preferred men.

Then he thanked me for the great favor that I'd done for him.

"You're most welcome," I told him, bewildered. I asked him if his family knew about this, and he answered that he waited for two years before daring to tell his mother. As for Maria, he told her the very same day, and she immediately burst out sobbing! After a few minutes, when she'd calmed down a little, she asked him if he believed in God. He asked her if she'd gone mad, but she kept repeating her question insistently until he said, "No!" His answer calmed her down a lot, and she said smiling, "Because if you'd been a believer, then you'd go to hell!"

She advised him that he needed to hide his homosexuality if he came to visit her in Ukraine, where there'd been a rise in homophonic nationalist groups that were constantly assaulting gays and committing the ugliest possible crimes against them.

. . .

At this time we were approaching an area that was being
shelled, so we stopped on the side of the road for a while
that felt like days to me, to wait for the attack to end. Ali
said to me, "I wish I could smoke!" I told him that my need
to go to the bathroom had chosen to come at this critical
moment, and I tried at first to forget it temporarily by
thinking about other things. But now my thoughts were
completely taken up with Ali's homosexuality. The news
of his gayness really bothered me, though normally I was
totally fine with gay people. I have lots of gay friends—my
friend Muhammad, for example. Sometimes he sleeps in
the same room with me, and there's no ambiguity about it
at all—there's no difference between him and any of my
girlfriends. But Ali is a different story. His homosexuality
dashed my hopes.

"Oh well!…" I said to myself.

Not long after this, I lost my ability even to think,
because my need to go to the bathroom put my mind in
a state of emergency! There was still shelling at that time,
so we weren't permitted to get off the bus. I was afraid
of losing control over my bladder and squeezed to keep
my urine in. My face flushed red, and Ali told me that I'd

47

become the same color as the license plates on Lebanese public vehicles.

When the Israeli warplanes finally finished their attack and we were allowed to get out, I said happily, "We've been liberated!" I rushed off the bus, found a secluded place, and relieved myself there. For the amount that it burned, I felt that it was no longer pee coming out of me but nuclear lemon juice. Then I noticed that Ali hadn't gotten off of the bus to smoke, and he seemed troubled. I wondered what was going on with him.

After we set off again, I realized that I'd left my purse where we'd stopped. It had all my official documents and a lot of cash in it. I hurried over to tell one of the embassy employees, pleading with them to let us go back and retrieve it. He refused, saying that security measures required the buses in our convoy to remain together. Besides, the roads were being shelled, and we couldn't just come and go on them as we pleased. This is when Ali intervened and was able to convince him that we needed to go back. Lucky for me, my purse was exactly where I'd left it.

• • •

Obviously that embassy employee had a high opinion of Ali's character because he made him responsible for collecting the passports of all the passengers on the bus and taking them to the Lebanese, and then the Syrian, security officials when we arrived at the border. He said to make sure not to lose any of them. But Ali refused this role and seemed way more worried about it than he should've been. I volunteered to take his place, saying to him, "Don't you think you're overexaggerating a bit?"

This contradiction in Ali's personality surprised me— he seemed strong inside the bus and weak outside of it. I wondered why he deliberately didn't get off the bus whenever we stopped, and in the end I asked him. But he changed the subject and asked me if I was hungry. I actually was hungry since it was now after two in the afternoon, and I had no food with me. He gave me some of what he'd brought with him.

While we were eating, I waited for him to finish talking about his homosexuality and explain in detail my role in it. I also expected him to justify his gayness to me, like every other gay person I'd known had done. They always said that their orientation was inborn, and therefore they were victims of biology, macho society, and these kinds of things. But Ali didn't say anything. No doubt he considered the subject closed, because he started eating his sandwich silently. This forced me to bring up the subject again and to clarify my tolerant position on homosexuality, since I was afraid of misunderstandings! So I started telling him about my friend Muhammad...

"Muhammad Ahmad?" he cut me off anxiously, saying that he knew him well, because they were friends when he was still living in Lebanon.

He added a bit angrily that Muhammad is unbearable because he's demanding, spoiled, and lazy. He also said that going out with him in public was a scandal! What he was saying was true, since going out with Muhammad actually was a scandal—every time we hung out together at night with my friends in a nightclub, he'd get drunk. Then he'd start provoking all of the guys there and throwing himself at them as though he were a ballet dancer with a big belly. The guys would ask us to get him off them or they'd hit him. Once his behavior even caused us to get thrown out of the club.

Ali told me that he'd met Muhammad at a party. He started going over to his house almost every day, and some of our school friends went with him sometimes.

I was shocked when he mentioned their names since I never would have believed that they were "that sort."

"Then expect it my girl," replied "Hajjeh" Ali.

He told me that they all used to watch gay porno films together and explore each other's bodies. But he didn't lose his virginity until he visited his sister in Ukraine later that summer, where he met an older man with whom he spent the most wonderful two months of his life. That whole time, his sister was terrified that someone would assault him, since his actions, words, and appearance all made it obvious that he was gay. When he announced his desire to move to Ukraine for good, so he could be near his boyfriend, she convinced their mother to make him return to Lebanon as quickly as possible.

But he couldn't bear to remain in Lebanon for long. After a year of trying, he convinced his mother to send him to live with one of her relatives in Germany.

His arrival in Germany was not a migration to the Promised Land. In his first week there, he visited the city's gay neighborhood and saw in broad daylight men wearing women's clothes, walking hand in hand. Then a transgendered prostitute gave him a cigarette. That

51

shocked him a lot, even though he'd seen similar things on television and on the Internet when he lived in Lebanon. After absorbing the shock for a few minutes, he suddenly sensed danger. Everything here in Germany was permissible, and everything was possible! He also felt a powerful feeling of disgust that forced him to vomit into one of the brilliant green trash cans nearby.

That visit was enough to keep him far away from the area for weeks. He spent his time searching for a life partner on Internet sites that specialized in introducing gay men. On these sites he met a lot of young men about whom he remembered very little. One of them once invited him to spend an evening together, where he met a man thirty years older than him who offered him a huge amount of drugs and took him to bed. This quickly became his first lover in Germany.

After a while, Ali left his mother's relative's house and moved to the gay neighborhood to be near to his new lover. He thought that their love would last forever, but it didn't even last until the end of that year since he soon discovered that his boyfriend was "cheating on him" with dozens of other young men.

"I was just one of his boys," he exclaimed angrily. "It was totally unacceptable!"

He said that to his boyfriend, who answered that he was free to do what he wanted, and if he didn't like it, no one was forcing him to stay.

"So did you stay?" I asked him, and he replied, "How could I stay? My dignity was at stake!"

He then added that this breakup was very difficult for him, especially since he'd gotten addicted to many kinds of drugs by then. His colleagues and professors at school came to know about this quickly and insisted that he check himself into rehab. He believed them, and so he decided at that very moment to move to a different neighborhood to start a new life.

He met his second love during his drug rehab treatments. He was British and worked in a law firm. Thanks to him, Ali was able to finally be free of his addiction. Their relationship lasted until his boyfriend was forced to move to California for his job. He asked Ali to go with him, but at that time Ali had applied for citizenship and was not permitted to travel for years. He kept dreaming that he would move to America and marry his boyfriend. This

play the role of psychotherapist, especially since the heat made the bus into a hell, and we were burning in it like infidels. But Ali didn't realize how annoyed I was with him and started to add something when my boyfriend called to check up on me.

Ali guessed who was calling and asked me as soon as I hung up if "society" limited my freedom to be alone with my boyfriend. So I told him about the period of time when I was living in my parents' house in Nabatiyyeh when we didn't have a place to go, except my boyfriend's grandmother's house. She'd lived alone since her husband died and had given my boyfriend the key to her house so he could sleep at her place sometimes. She was still very healthy and went out every day to do her errands. We knew exactly when she would go out and come back, so we would "visit her" when she was out. But she surprised us more than once by coming back before she was supposed to, and I hid in the wardrobe. One of these times I was forced to stuff myself into the shoe cupboard. I got into a position that caused me back pains for days. I preferred that to her discovering that we'd been alone there and reporting it back to everyone she knew.

"Silly girl…" Ali said dismissively, because he'd expected to hear more serious things from me, things that the smell of blood and misery would waft out from. He asked me what I'd do if my liberated behaviors put my life in danger. I settled on smiling and didn't answer, so he asked if his life would be in danger if he moved back to Lebanon.

"Everything's possible!" I answered jokingly.

I had wanted to finish with this topic as quickly as possible because the heat had started suffocating me, and my thirst was making me practically swallow my tongue. My thirst increased whenever I talked. As for the tiny bit of water I had left, I preferred to not drink it for fear that it would make me have to go to the bathroom. My answer caused the desired effect, because Ali drowned in his thoughts. I took advantage of the opportunity to appear as though I wanted to sleep, and actually did doze off.

• • •

A short while later, voices of travelers woke me, insisting that an embassy employee turn on the air conditioning because the heat had become unbearable. But he refused, protesting that there was hardly any diesel left in the fuel tank. One of the ladies retorted that her elderly mother sitting near us was suffering from blood pressure

56

problems and that the heat had made her pass out. The embassy employee replied, "Madame! Have you forgotten that we are war refugees? Do you think we're on a bus tour?"

That answer quieted Madame down, as well as the rest of the passengers who were also about to protest. Everyone sat in silence for a few moments, except the little girl who started saying over and over again to her mother that she felt hot and thirsty. Ali got up from his seat and gave her all the water he had with him. This succeeded in quieting her down, but not for long because, soon after, she started repeating that she needed to go to the bathroom. It didn't take her long to respond to this need, and the smell started wafting through the bus.

Her mother changed her diaper. But she didn't get rid of it by throwing it out the window, because she was against throwing trash onto the road, on principle. This angered one of the women sitting near her. She said that a few days ago, Israeli planes had bombed the electricity plant in Jiyyeh, setting the fuel stores on fire, releasing massive amounts of poison gas into the atmosphere, and causing hundreds of barrels of oil to spill into the sea. Did this lady think that she'd save the environment by not throwing one diaper onto the road and forcing us to breathe in her daughter's "poison gas"? Before the woman could answer, a fighter plane roared by above us. The passengers got upset and sat silently still. With this disturbance, the woman threw the diaper out the open window. It flew far, crashed into the barbed wire surrounding one of the agricultural fields, and hung there like a holiday decoration.

"A gift from the Russians to Lebanon!" Ali said. The woman told him to shut up.

. . .

During the subsequent hour, we stopped many times without being allowed to get out, because from time to time we would come to areas being shelled. Ali continually reiterated his strong craving for a cigarette. Finally, I asked him angrily, "Why didn't you get off the bus when it was allowed?" But he didn't reply and changed the subject, wondering aloud if it was possible for a missile to hit us by mistake. Then he asked me, "If it happened and it hit us, do you think that we'd feel anything before we died?" I begged him to stop slipping into exaggerations and to spare me the flights of his expansive imagination.

. . .

Sitting on the bus for long hours had exhausted most of the evacuees, especially the woman who was eight months pregnant and who'd started walking up and down the aisle to relieve her swollen legs.

When we arrived in Tripoli, the calm atmosphere there surprised us. No targets had been bombed there for several days, and the swimming pools, cafes, and streets were full of people as if the war was happening in another, faraway country. I wondered at that moment if I'd made the right decision in leaving this city to go to my grandmother's house in Russia.

My grandmother has been ill for more than ten years, and her health has worsened recently, to the point that she didn't recognize me when I visited her last year. She thought I was a German army conscript from the Second World War and that I was holding her hostage in her home. She completely refused to eat for fear that the food was poisoned. She started waiting until I went to sleep each night to escape from her apartment wearing her nightdress. Every morning, the neighbors would find her lost in the street and bring her back home. I tried to lock the door at night, but it did no good because she knew how to open it. In the end, I moved to my aunt's house and stayed there until it was time to return to Lebanon. After this, my mother hired a nurse to live with my grandmother full time and look after her. Now the time had come for her yearly holiday, and my aunt offered to take her place. But our coming changed the program, and the job of nursing her fell to us.

This is what I told Ali. He said that he also was hesitant to go to Ukraine, though he really missed his grandmother and siblings, because he would be forced to complete military service there. Then he hit his cheek with the palm of his hand like the women in Nabatiyyeh do, saying, "Oh my… a pansy in the army!" Then he got lost in his own thoughts.

After a period of silence, he suddenly grabbed my arm and said that if he didn't smoke right this minute, he'd die! I answered, "And I'll die if I don't pee!"

But both of us were forced to suppress our needs until we approached the Lebanese-Syrian border at last. We stopped moving because cars and buses were queued up there for kilometers. We were allowed to get off our bus until further notice, provided we didn't go too far away, since it had rapidly became clear to the embassy employees that we wouldn't reach the border checkpoint for hours. Everyone got off, with the exception of Ali.

He urged me to stay with him on the bus, but I refused because I desperately had to use the bathroom and it was unbearably hot inside the bus. I wondered why he was staying on the bus, despite this lethal heat, and I tried to convince him to come outside, unsuccessfully. I asked him, "Is there something outside that is scaring you that much?" But he didn't reply, opened the window, and lit a cigarette, saying happily, "I almost died of deprivation!"

. . .

The region in which we stopped was desert-like—there wasn't even one tree, and the few bushes there were yellow and shriveled. The people living there were a group of gypsies, who'd set up their tents a few meters from the road. When we arrived, they were tending a herd of goats and speaking to them in a language we didn't understand. They let us use their "bathroom." This bathroom was a small tent, set a bit apart from the others, from which a terrible smell emerged since thousands of evacuees had used it before us. In exchange, we were meant to buy something from their "shop," i.e., a broken table that had bags of chips past their expiration date, chocolate bars that the heat had turned into a drink, and a pack of cigarettes.

It was actually the cigarettes that my mother was short on, since she had finished her last one hours ago, but she refused to buy it from them because she was afraid that they might be decayed. Cigarettes were something she needed, because it was the one way for her to keep her nerves steady until the end of the journey. My mother wasn't afraid of bombs or warplanes, but this long bus journey had made her really anxious.

Then we saw from a distance what looked to us like a small village next to the road, not far from the border. We decided to walk over to it. Perhaps we'd find what we needed there. My mother's friend and her nearly naked daughters joined us, and when we had moved a bit away from them, Ali stuck his head out of one the windows and called out to me, "Hey woman!"

He asked me to get on the bus with him. I asked him sarcastically what he was hiding from on the bus and continued walking with the others.

One of the girls asked me who he was, and I told her his name. She immediately knew who he was because she'd been in school with us. She said that she remembered his enthusiasm during demonstrations against Israel, when his voice would rise above everyone else's, and he'd compel everyone around him to repeat after him the slogans he'd made up. She added that she respected strong men like him because they were the only ones who defended the nation's honor. Then she remembered as well that Ali had beaten up one of the boys in her class once, sending him to the hospital because he'd said that Israel had a right to exist.

She was about to add something else, but the comments of the young men we were passing by prevented her. At that moment we were crossing through an area where the Russian buses were lined up, and we started walking past the cars and buses full of other people trying to leave who immediately noticed her exposed legs.

• • •

The village's main square was so teeming with people that nothing was left to drink in the shop except alcohol. The shopkeeper reassured us that he'd sent workers into Syria to bring back more merchandise, but we couldn't wait so we took two bottles of warm beer and a payphone card, and left.

A lot of people were lined up outside the payphone. When it was the turn of the old woman wearing a hijab standing in front of us, she started crying loudly because her call was to her son who was trapped under bombardment with his family. Many of the people waiting behind us were about to start crying with her.

Then it was my mother's turn. She called my father and spoke to him in Russian so that none of the non-Russians standing around us could understand what she was saying. He told her that he'd arrived in Nabatiyyeh a little while before.

My mother's call lasted no more than a few minutes, and quite a few units were left on the card. So I took it from her and called my boyfriend. But I wasn't able to speak to him much, because the people standing behind me were starting to pay attention to every word that I said. Seconds were long enough for them to realize that I wasn't saying anything "important" and that I was therefore delaying them from their important calls to their relatives. They started acting resentful, and I knew that I had to either start crying or hang up. I decided to hang up.

At that moment, a terrible thundering noise rang out in the air! Everyone rushed to hide in entrances to homes or ran back to buses and cars. The village square was quickly emptied of people. Only my mother remained standing in this place as though nothing was happening, because she realized immediately that we were not in danger. The thundering noise was from breaking the sound barrier, not the roar of a warplane. My mother had spent half her life on an air force base because her father was a pilot in the Soviet Army.

A few moments were enough for things in the square to return to normal. The people in nearby houses had moved their televisions onto the balcony, and we could easily hear the news about the war broadcast on them. We knew that a few areas were at that moment under continual, indiscriminate bombardment and that the number of civilian deaths and injuries was rising every minute.

Then Ali's family came to the square, his sister's face flushed with tears. I remembered that Ali was still sitting in the bus and felt guilty for leaving him alone, so I took the two bottles of beer and left, on the pretext that I'd forgotten my mobile phone there.

But before I left the village, I decided to go to the bathroom in one of the houses so I wouldn't be forced to do it on the road afterwards. The woman of the house let me in and welcomed me, leading me to the bathroom, which was occupied at that moment, so I waited outside the door for it to be empty. The voices of women talking in Russian rose from behind it. From what they were saying, I understood that they were prostitutes coming to take care of their needs here. One of them had stuffed her bra with little plastic bags inflated with air, and when she bent over to clean her shoe, one of these bags had slipped and fallen on the floor. Her friend stepped on it by accident and her high-heeled shoe sunk into it, making it pop loudly. One of her breasts was then much larger than the other, so all she could do was stuff her bra with a huge amount of tissue.

• • •

At first I didn't see Ali on the bus because he was hiding between the seats. He seemed upset and informed me that Maria's husband had sent his two brothers to follow the evacuation and bring his sister and her daughter back home by force. He saw them walking between the evacuation buses and immediately knew who they were and what they wanted. He was afraid they would hurt him, so he rushed back to hide. He asked me to go to the village square to warn his mother and sister.

As soon as I conveyed this news to them, Maria started trembling from her head down to her toes, saying, "They're going to slaughter me like a sheep on Eid!"

Her mother told Maria to quiet down and hide in one of the village houses with her daughter, then she relayed what happened to one of the embassy employees, who answered dismissively that she was certainly exaggerating.

Soon after, Maria's two brothers-in-law arrived in the square dragging Ali behind them. They threatened his mother that they would hurt him if she didn't meet their demands! An embassy employee got involved then, saying that Maria had official permission from her husband to travel with her daughter and that they had no right to force her to return. He ordered them to release Ali immediately. But this didn't stop them from repeating their threats, so the employee summoned the embassy's guard over to us. That frightened the two brothers, and they freed Ali, left the square, and didn't come back.

When Ali and I got back to the bus, he lit a cigarette saying, "My sister's like a tennis ball, this situation is totally unstable!"

From on the bus, we saw Maria. She was afraid and asked the embassy employees for her passport back so she could return to Nabatiyyeh. They refused, saying that they'd now become responsible for her and couldn't allow her to leave the caravan. But she kept insisting, crying until her mother came and scolded her.

Ali commented on what we'd seen, saying that he didn't understand why Maria acted that way, when she'd finally gotten what she'd been hoping for. She should be happy, especially since her daughter would visit her second country, Ukraine, for the first time. She would finally learn her grandmother's language after these two things had been forbidden to her previously because her father was afraid that a "Russian" mentality would be transmitted to her—not merely through the language alone but also through the films and TV broadcasts that come to Lebanon from Russia and Ukraine by satellite, and which his mother-in-law watched all the time. For this reason, he imposed strict censorship on everything watched at home on TV. He only allowed the watching of Arab and Turkish shows and soaps. He also forbade his wife and her mother to speak "Russian" in front of their daughter. In this way he defied his mother-in-law, trying to establish that he was the man of the house, despite her paying their monthly rent. He was unable to provide for his family, making him feel a huge shortcoming in his masculinity. Maria disobeyed his orders once and started secretly teaching her daughter "Russian," and when he learned about it, he beat her.

"That pansy!" Ali said angrily.

. . .

I lost my ability to listen to him at this point because it had gotten so hot. I interrupted him, begging him to get out of the bus with me so we could find somewhere else to sit. But he insisted on remaining, protesting that he wanted to keep listening to the news on the bus's radio, since his digital player didn't have a radio. He asked me to stay with him, and I stayed because he seemed really anxious.

He got more anxious with every new bit of news we heard. The radio announced that Israel had shelled a twelve-story building on the pretext that one of Hezbollah's offices was located there. More than forty civilians who lived there were killed. It also announced that it had bombed a bus that had a number of families fleeing from the South, scattering the bodies of fathers, mothers, and children burnt to bits. Blood was flowing on the roads like a river. Moreover, Israel was continually bombarding Beirut's southern suburbs, targeting water and fuel supplies, as well as bridges and seaports. This morning, it had bombed the Beirut-Damascus Road and killed three civilians just as they were crossing the Lebanese-Syrian border. It threatened to bomb the northern border where we were stopped at this very moment.

Then the radio broadcast played interviews with the families of the martyrs and people living in areas under bombardment who said that they would remain steadfast in the face of the wrathful enemy. They said they wouldn't rest until the blood of the Jews was shed and flowed like rivers!

Ali shuddered at this, and his fear reached its apex. I wondered what had frightened him so much, and I turned off the radio. I suggested that he drink the beer that I'd bought, thinking that perhaps it would calm him down a bit. But he refused, saying that he had to remain alert and aware, in order to protect himself from any plot to murder him. I laughed but he glowered at me and said that he'd decided to disclose one of his biggest secrets to me. He came so close to me that he was hanging on to my body and told me about the summer when he turned fourteen years old. That year he went to Ukraine to visit his grandmother, as he did every summer. One day, he was bored of playing with his friends in the neighborhood and took advantage of his grandmother going out to the market to search through her cupboards for something to entertain himself, even though he wasn't allowed to open the cupboards. In one of them he found an old Torah that his grandmother had hidden from him. It was then that he knew his grandmother was Jewish. This meant his mother was Jewish, and therefore he was Jewish too because lineage in Judaism is passed through the mother!

He covered his face with his hands, blushed all the way to the tips of his ears, and seemed to be on the verge of crying.

"It's not a big deal," I told him.

But it was a big deal to him, especially since now we were at war with Israel. He had been afraid of the people working at the border crossing knowing that his mother was Jewish from her family name, listed in her passport. It was also printed in both of her children's passports, putting all of them in grave danger! He said this, then threw his arms in the air shouting, "They'll murder us like dogs!"

Then he thought a bit and added, "Or, rather, like pigs."

I suppressed an urge to giggle and begged him not to be silly. How would people working at border security know anything about Russian family names, Jewish or otherwise? This didn't calm him down much, and signs of serious anxiety remained etched on his face.

He was just about to say something when we heard a loud scream, followed by a powerful noise. An elderly woman had been standing in front of our bus, when one of the young men ran over her foot with his bicycle. She had fallen down from the intense pain, and everything in her purse scattered all over the ground. I immediately went out to help her. She insisted that I hurry up and collect her Russian papers that were strewn all around for fear that the goats, which were at that moment grazing by the side of the road, would eat them.

Her mobile phone had also fallen under the bus. When I bent down to retrieve it, I heard the sound of the engine being turned on, so I jumped up from where I was, terrified that the bus had started moving and would crush me under its wheels. Ali realized what was happening and laughed at me because the sound actually was coming from a nearby car.

· · ·

The embassy employees announced that the convoy would start moving soon, and they gave me a list of names of the passengers on the bus, asking me to locate each one of them and inform them that they needed to return to their seats. After this, I had to accompany one of the embassy employees to the Lebanese border security post to give them all the passengers' passports.

At border security, a man standing in line in front of me asked me if I was Russian. I pointed at my passport without answering. He told me in Russian, in an accent that I could barely understand, that he'd specialized in medicine in Moscow, and he now was practicing in one of the villages in the Beqaa. When I didn't answer at all, he said that Russian women were the most beautiful women in the world. Or that is what he meant to say, but because he had trouble pronouncing the Russian word for "beautiful"—substituting one letter for another— he unintentionally said that Russian women were the world's sports shoes. I laughed, then I explained his mistake to him in Arabic. He was amazed at my ability to speak Arabic so fluently, and so I told him that my father was Lebanese, and I had lived in Lebanon my whole life. He said, "It's like you're Jewish!" By this he meant that I'd betrayed him because I let him speak Russian, though he didn't know it well, and made himself a target of ridicule.

We spent a long time at Lebanese border control because some people's official paperwork was incomplete. In the end we found solutions to all of the problems. When I got back on the bus, the sun had started setting, and I was really exhausted. I didn't notice that Ali was avoiding looking at me, until he asked me how I'd been thinking about him since he confessed to his mother's Jewishness. He didn't give me a chance to answer, adding, "Don't you dare think that I've embraced Judaism!"

He announced that for him the welfare of his homeland came before everything else and that he was prepared to die for even just a handful of Lebanon's soil!

He asked me not to tell anyone about this. "I beg of you!" he said to me.

• • •

His previous experiences in this matter had been really troubling. For example, he had told our friend Muhammad about his "Jewishness" when he was still living in Lebanon, after Muhammad had promised to keep it totally secret. But they fought not long after this, and our friend threatened to spread the news to everyone he knew! He actually did tell two of our classmates, who forced Ali to buy their silence temporarily, with money and gifts, until he emigrated to Germany two months later.

I told him not to worry, because no one would really care, and that he was making things a much bigger deal than they deserved to be. And in any case, he wasn't Jewish, according to his father's religion. Even if he was Jewish, and the border officials knew about it, they wouldn't harm him. But he didn't answer.

• • •

We stopped in front of the inspection checkpoint, following the Syrian border control. A Syrian officer got on the bus to examine the travelers' faces. As soon as Ali saw him, he covered his face with his hands and pretended that he was sleeping!

Afterwards, the embassy employee asked me to take the passports to the Syrian border security building. When I'd carried out his orders and come back onto the bus about a quarter of an hour later, Ali was no longer separation made him go back to his previous lifestyle. He almost became addicted again, but he succeeded in staying steady.

Then he said that his emotional torment had never affected his studies or work. He was always first in his class at school and university. He studied medicine for a few months following his mother's wishes, but he quickly changed his mind and switched to communications. Now he works in one of the most important local television stations and in his spare time volunteers at an old people's home. But he started to lose his ability to separate work and relationships recently because his overpowering sense of loneliness compelled him to go out with many young men whose names he couldn't even remember. This depleted his energy, and he almost lost his job. This is one of the reasons for his desire to return to Lebanon, since he thought that living here would inevitably force him to be more disciplined.

• • •

"Isn't that so?" he asked me, expecting me to agree with him. But I didn't answer. His continuous nagging annoyed me, and I felt that he was pelting me with his problems as if he were stoning me. I wasn't prepared to covering his face. I asked him to stop exaggerating because his increasing anxiety had started to annoy me.

Then he put his earphones in angrily and started listening to Fairouz, enjoying her songs which were all about her nationalism. But his player's batteries soon ran out, and he couldn't recharge it except in an electrical outlet.

. . .

An hour passed without them giving the passports back to us. The entire time, Ali was preoccupied by his fear of being targeted. This is exactly what he said to me when I asked him what was up. He closed the curtains over the windows so that no one outside could see him and made a narrow opening, through which he started surveilling everything that was happening. Whenever anyone stopped near our bus, he held the edge of the curtain in his clenched fist. He only relaxed when they left. He stayed like this for hours, until the passports were distributed to their owners, and then he said, "Thank God!"

But we didn't set off right away, as we had expected, because the passport of a Ukrainian lady sitting on our bus was missing. She started searching for it in her purse—perhaps she had left it there without realizing it. But she couldn't find it. We got angry at this delay because there still was a long, tiring journey ahead of us. We still had to get to the Lattakia airport and from there to Moscow, and then we had to get to our families' houses wherever they were located all throughout Russia and the countries of the former Soviet Union.

We then learned that Maria and Ali's mother's passports were also missing. One of the employees went to border security to investigate, and he asked me to go with him to translate. After a lot of back and forth, they sent us to an office, and the Syrian official there got really angry at us because we'd dared to accuse him of losing passports. He shouted in our faces that it was impossible.

All the while, Israel was renewing its threat to bomb the northern border between Lebanon and Syria. The employees decided that we should set off right away. They asked the women who'd lost their passports to leave the convoy, rather than risking the lives of all of the travelers. This filled Ali's mother with rage, and she told them that she wouldn't leave the evacuation convoy no matter what happened.

• • •

When I got back on the bus, Ali whispered to me, "We're finished!"

He passed his fingers across his neck, indicating that it would be slashed open. I answered that the missing passports had nothing to do with his mother's Jewishness, because for the Syrian officials on the border, we all were Russian citizens, nothing more. Our sectarian affiliations were the least of their worries. Lots of Jews visit Lebanon, Syria, and other Arab countries with no problem—diplomats, journalists, and foreign tourists. He asked me, "Even if they are Israelis?"

I asked him what he meant by that. Whispering, he informed me that his grandmother was one of the people rescued from the German massacres of Jews during the Second World War. The German army raided her house and arrested all the members of her family. At that time, she'd been out in the nearby forest gathering firewood, and so she was spared. After the establishment of the state of Israel, she received financial compensation, as reparations for the harm caused to her. She sent a big part of that compensation to her daughter in Lebanon. Israel had offered citizenship to his grandmother and her children, and invited them to settle there. But they refused. No doubt one of the officials at the border had learned of this somehow and had hid their passports so the evacuation convoy would continue on without them. Then they were going to lead them to a dark corner somewhere and take revenge on them.

I asked him sarcastically, "Take revenge on you?" He replied in all seriousness, "Like dogs!" I rejoined, "What about the Ukrainian woman? Is her passport lost because she's Jewish too?"

But Ali didn't answer. He thought a little and said that the only solution to the problem is that the three women enter Syria using their Lebanese identity cards and get a visa to enter Russia in the Moscow airport. Then they can go to the Ukrainian embassy in Moscow, get new passports, and finally return to their country.

I proposed this solution to the embassy employees. They found it ideal. But Ali's mother had left her Lebanese passport and ID card at home, and she had no more official papers with her, proving who she was. This would prevent her from entering Syria or Russia, and even returning to Lebanon. She was trapped at the border!

She urged the employees to go back and try to find the passports at the border control office. I responded to her pleas. As soon as I entered the building, I found the passports thrown on a chair. I grabbed them and hurried out.

When Ali's mother saw me she shouted with great joy, "Allahu Akbar!"

She hugged me to her, ramming my head into her giant bosom. But I couldn't stand being so close to her and quickly got her off of me. Then I asked one of the employees if I could change my seat on the bus. He said no, and I went back and sat down next to Ali out of obligation.

"Welcome neighbor!" Ali said greeting me upon my return. He wanted to kiss me, but I moved away from him.

He sighed and then told me without me asking that he detected a strange smell wafting off of his mother and grandmother when he found out they were Jewish. This scent was really nasty, so at the beginning he couldn't stand to be really close to them. But the smell started to dissipate as time passed, and now he doesn't notice it, except rarely.

. . .

What Ali was saying reminded me of an Israeli film that I had seen some time ago at the suggestion of one of my classmates. He'd bought it on one of his trips abroad. The film opens with a scene of a devout Jewish man who was getting ready to leave his house in the morning. He got out of bed, washed his face and hands as though purifying himself for prayer, then started putting on traditional clothes. The thing I remember most is that he put on perfume, or perhaps I imagined that.

Perhaps I was afraid that Ali himself would start to emit the fragrance of perfume, indeed I imagined that I actually smelled it. I felt it was being released from his pores, mouth, ears, and nostrils, from behind his eyelids. This scent started growing stronger and stronger, until I imagined that it was assaulting my nose. My feelings horrified me, as did what I was imagining. I was overcome by the need to vomit and hoped that the bus might stop right then. But the bus didn't stop, and I remained imprisoned in my seat, about to suffocate.

And this is how I remained until my need to pee eclipsed any other feeling and extinguished the flames of my torment. This only intensified, and hours later when we'd finally reached the Lattakia airport, I felt like I was about to explode. Many other evacuees were in the same situation, since we'd been imprisoned inside buses for more than twelve hours in a row.

• • •

Volunteers from the Syrian Red Cross met us outside the airport and offered us apples and bottled water. We asked them where the bathrooms were, and they pointed to a door behind the airport building. A grassy plot of land separated us from it. There were only a few toilets in the bathroom for our large numbers. It was late at night, and the strip of land before us was unlit. Many people just peed straightaway on the grass. A car passed in front of us and lit up the area with its lights. For a brief moment I saw a huge number of white bums, shining in front of me like full moons on a clear night. Then they disappeared.

But they appeared once again, because the very same car returned with its lights shining. One of the women threw a dirty diaper at it. The diaper stuck to the car's front window and the wipers couldn't scrape it off. Other women threw water bottles at it like stones. This prompted it to drive away and not come back.

Ali got out of the bus against his will and peed without noticing that there was a woman squatting on the grass in front of him. He didn't see her because it was extremely dark. The woman started waving her hands, trying to get him away from her but hit him between the legs by accident. He collapsed on the ground in terrible pain, shouting, "Leave me alone!"

As for me, peeing was very painful because I'd held it in for such a long time. I felt such terrible pain that it was not like peeing but a letting of blood! My eyes teared up, but I was determined not to cry.

After we finished the peeing party, we took our suitcases from the buses and headed for the airport.

• • •

The airport was a medium-sized room that had a number of desks and border control booths at the end of it. We only had to walk across this room to board the planes headed for Moscow. The airport was really small relative to our huge numbers, but this didn't prevent us all from entering in one push. We squeezed ourselves in like livestock. Everyone was afraid there wouldn't be enough seats on the planes for all the travelers and started shoving each other violently in front of the border control gate, because everyone wanted to pass through it first.

Ali was able to locate me in the throng and asked me if I missed Lebanon. But he didn't give me a chance to answer, telling me that he felt estranged because we were far from the coast and that he couldn't see the sea. This is one of the main reasons that he hated the city where he lived in Germany. The sunset there was very strange because it went down in the middle of the evening. Since it didn't set behind the sea, it looked like a fried egg! Indifferently, I told him that Lattakia was actually on the coast. He thought a bit, then replied that being far from Lebanon caused him unbearable suffering nonetheless.

. . .

Ali's suffering was the least of my worries at that moment because I was so terribly hungry that my stomach had started to digest itself. I didn't answer him, especially as it wasn't time to chat, because all around us the pushing and shoving travelers had almost crushed us.

One of the ladies pulled Ali by his shirt to move him out of her way. He screamed, believing that the airport guards were arresting him. He then told me that he felt he was being surveilled and targeted, and as soon as he said that, one of the workers pushed him aside and said, "Let the lady pass!"

By "lady," he meant the prostitute whose hand he was holding. He was clearing a path for her through the throng, helping her cross to the gate for passport inspection and delivering her right to the aircraft. A number of the prostitutes got through the crowd in the same way, making one of the "normal" women so angry that she shouted that little children had not had anything to eat or drink for hours, that old women were about to pass out from exhaustion, but they could only find "whores" to help? But the worker didn't reply and kept smiling. Then he went over to Ali's mother and whispered something into her ear. She slapped him hard and ordered him to get away from her—if not, she'd skewer him like a kabab.

• • •

A bit later, after one group of travelers had boarded an airplane that then took off to Moscow, the embassy employees closed the passport inspection gate without giving any reason. Many travelers objected to this, and the employees told them that they were free to leave the evacuation if they didn't like it.

Ali told me that he'd been craving a cigarette for a while but was afraid to smoke it outside. I suggested that we go to the cafeteria on the second floor of the building, since we might also find something to eat there. But the cafeteria only served cheese rolled up in stale bread sandwiches. I preferred not to eat.

When we sat down at one of the tables, Ali started saying that he was regretting not staying in Lebanon. At that same moment the television broadcast the song, "Death to Israel." He shuddered and begged me in a whisper not to tell anyone what he'd disclosed to me about his Russian grandmother and her relationship to Israel. He added that no one in Lebanon knew about this but me.

"Even your brother-in-law?" I asked him. He replied, "Especially my brother-in-law!"

He told me that Maria had decided to hide this from her husband from when they first met. Her husband had told her at the time that his brother was martyred while carrying out a combat mission in Israel. He remarked once that her mother's name was Jewish, but Maria persuaded him that her mother had converted to Islam when she married her father. Ali added that his sister's husband didn't know anything about their family or its history, and didn't know that the money that his mother-in-law paid for their rent was Israeli money.

. . .

Ali said all this whispering in Russian and wanted to add something else. But one of the cafeteria workers came over to him at that moment and asked him if he had a cigarette. Ali was nervous at first, and then he took a packet of cigarettes out of his pocket. The worker took one. His hand touched Ali's lightly. After a moment, the worker came back and asked him for another cigarette. Ali gave it to him and seemed anxious, so I asked him what was going on. He told me that he was surely there to spy on them. I begged him not to exaggerate. Then the worker came back a third time and asked Ali if he wanted to smoke a cigarette with him outside. Ali was upset because he thought the worker was luring him to a secluded place to hurt him. That's what he told me in Russian before getting up and leaving the cafeteria running. I rushed after him.

In the airport's main hall, Ali had "hidden" in the throng of travelers sitting on their suitcases, waiting for the passport inspection gates to open and let them board the planes. Only my mother's friend's daughter was standing motionless, her naked thighs gripping each other. When I asked her what was wrong, she told me that she'd gotten her period the moment they'd stepped into the airport and couldn't find a sanitary napkin or paper tissues. All she could do was try to block the flow of blood by clenching her thighs against each other. Ali noticed this and said, "The blood's reached your knees!"

He gave her one of his sweaters to wipe her blood with. Then one of the embassy employees asked us if anyone was a gynecologist, because the pregnant woman traveling with us had started to deliver. The woman refused the employee's suggestion to go to a nearby hospital because she didn't have enough money with her for that and also because she was afraid of the evacuation leaving without her and being left alone in Syria. She was lying down in one of the airport offices, but to her bad luck none of us was a gynecologist.

Not much later, the pregnant woman started screaming from her intense pain, her voice echoing off the airport walls. This created a commotion among the travelers, and Ali said, "Thank God I can't get pregnant!"

One of the women doctors started preparing for the woman to give birth and asked someone to assist her. Ali volunteered because he'd studied medicine at university for a few months, and he'd also helped his grandmother deliver one of the calves on her farm. But he quickly regretted his decision, because he soon became afraid that delivering this baby would provide a pretext for somehow deceiving him in order to lure him to a secluded room and finish him off.

"What if they'd killed me?" He whispered. I answered sarcastically, "Like dogs?"

But he didn't answer because the pregnant woman's screams intensified at that moment, and the doctor rushed over to help her, dragging Ali behind her. She kept screaming for a long time. After a while, I could feel her voice ringing in my ears like an ambulance's siren. The screams intensified with the passing of time, until they reached a crescendo, right when one of the airport employees entered the office to search for a file he needed, and then another had to use the only fax machine in the airport, which just happened to be located in that very room.

• • •

Ali didn't leave the office until very late at night. The gates for passport inspection were still closed, and we dozed off on the ground or on our suitcases waiting for them to open. Ali woke me to tell me that the woman had given birth to a boy who she named after him. Then he sighed, struck his cheek with his hand, and said, "Oh my!"

He clarified this statement by saying he'd suffered a lot in Germany because of his name. For the German authorities, it was a terrorist name, and he'd thought for years about changing it for another, more Russian one. He tried to convince the woman to choose another name for her son, but she insisted.

He sighed again and lit a cigarette, though it was forbidden to smoke in the airport hall. He started silently and warily surveilling everyone around us. When he'd been quiet for a while, I went back to sleep. But he woke me up again and asked me to go with him to the bathroom because he was afraid to go alone. He wanted to go with me into the women's room, but the cleaning woman sitting in front of it wouldn't let him. He spent a long time in the men's room, and when he finally came out and we went back to the main airport hall, I thought I noticed the young man from the cafeteria also coming out of it.

When we got back and sat down in front of our suitcases, Ali told me in a whisper that from the day he'd opened his grandmother's cupboard, he'd started feeling that he was in exile wherever he went. He sighed, lit a cigarette, and added that he was embarrassed to be leaving Lebanon and not defending it against its enemies.

· · ·

In the morning, the gates for passport inspection opened. We all had reached such levels of thirst and hunger that we rushed onto the airplanes as though they were the way to reach heaven. Despite his intense hunger, Ali wouldn't eat anything on the plane because he was afraid that it was poisoned. I was annoyed by his excessive paranoia and anxiety. I expressed this to him, apologized because I was exhausted, and fell right asleep. He tried to wake me up a number of times, but I didn't react.

· · ·

As soon as we got off the airplane in the Moscow airport, volunteers from the Russian Rescue Association offered us sandwiches and bottles of water. Ali finally submitted to his hunger, took a sandwich, and ate it quickly and hungrily. A second later, he noticed that it contained pork, rushed to the bathroom, and vomited it up. I told him that I found this behavior strange, and I told him so. He responded that he couldn't stand to eat pork, because from childhood he'd been forbidden to eat it.

• • •

After we crossed through the passport control point at the Moscow Airport and entered the arrivals hall, we found a throng of journalists working for a number of local and international channels waiting for us. I quickly moved away from them. But Ali cut a path through the crowd gathered around, and when he succeeded in getting their attention he said angrily in Russian that he came from South Lebanon, and it was being destroyed by Israeli shelling. He said that he hated Israel to the death and hoped it would burn in hell! He said that resisting it was the duty of every honorable person, exactly like the Soviet resistance to the brutal German occupiers had been a duty for every honorable person in the Soviet Union and the whole world.

His face flushed red as tomato paste, and he lifted his finger in the air, screaming in anger that Israel had desecrated the purity of our land, raped our country, and spilled the blood of our innocent children, and that he wouldn't rest until they were expelled from every inch of our country.

His words became increasingly emotional as he cried out, "Those dogs!" His eyes teared up as he added, "Those pigs!"

With that, he started coughing. When it had been going on for a while, the journalists started talking to other travelers. After he'd calmed down, he tried to get their attention again, but with no success.

• • •

The next day, I watched the news on several television channels that broadcast detailed reports on the evacuation. But none of them included any of what Ali had shouted.

I was twenty-one when I realized that my mother was an immigrant. From her Soviet hometown on the cusp of Finland, too far north for Genghis Khan's dissemination to cloud the rare Slavic purity of its inhabitants' blood—so the legend goes—she journeyed southward to Moscow, where she blemished the purity of her race with that of a fellow student from a godforsaken Arab country, whose tongue slipped on the iced curves of Cyrillic letters and who eventually returned to this "Lebanon," a dot jumbled in the ebb and flow of surrounding national borders, hugged by the warm waters of the Mediterranean. She came with him, of course. And so did I, the jug in which their wines intermingled.

Why did it take me twenty-one years to unravel that simple ball of yarn? Perhaps it was a symptom of things less simple: entanglements of belonging, the nebulous nature of feeling at home. Roots slither under the ground, intertwining where our eyes are unable to map them. Of course, I knew exactly where my mother's roots were, she was Russian—for me she had never been anything else—but part of the reason that her immigrant status evaded me even as I chewed on its bitter fruit was that one does not really immigrate to Lebanon. Migrant workers from the Global South live and die marred in their exclusion, their children never holding the keys to the garden (how do *they* define their identities?). Visitors from the higher end of the global table feel the heat of reality from under the extended roofs of their foreign passports. The human sediments of refugee communities continue to live as ghosts on the plot of the nation. To me, my mother was more of an expatriate from the Soviet Union than anything else, but an expatriate who was grafted into the legal fabric of the country by virtue of marrying a Lebanese man (only men pass on citizenship, let alone social identity). She always had the full rights of a (female) national; she could even run for the parliament if she so wished. It was the social fabric of the country that my mother never found enough thread to seamlessly stitch herself into, or perhaps she had no desire to push the needle too many times into her flesh.

This fluid rigidity of my mother's identity must have been what confused me.

Her immediate transplantation into the orchard of patrilineage was met with a codified cultural firmness, a sort of essentialism emanating, pheromone-like, from her pores, later reabsorbed in the form of fertilized platitudes thrown at her feet. As it was, she always had one foot in each door. Although these things never crossed the synapses between my eye and my tongue, I saw her languish in the language of custom, her mimicry of social rites forever smacking of theatricality. And it is precisely this theatricality that flows under the transparent surface of *Ali and His Russian Mother*—I see this now that I have reread it, in English translation, six years later (I must confess that no such things crossed my mind at the time that I wrote the novel).

Ali's mother, of course, has nothing to do with my own, just as none of the characters have to do with me, in the blunt sense of the word. The rivers of relevance run deeper: immigration, from its makeshift seat in the sidelines, decentered and denaturalized seemingly essential positions, ones I had to pretend to have swallowed with my mother's milk. The child of an immigrant, I had a sort of double vision, both inside and outside, familiarized and foreign, simultaneously belonging to both my parents' realms and to neither. And with that came the liberating— and uncanny— realization of a sublime randomness, the randomness of forming allegiances and identities, of landing on one side of a conflict or on the other, whether it were military or any other.

Looking back, in much less anger, I think that I wrote *Ali* because I was trying, desperately, to emancipate myself from set forms of identity. In Lebanon, where I felt I had spent the entirety of my life, I walked within a glass mold, just like everyone else, waiting to fill in its shape with the years I gathered under its crust. My religion, my family, and my gender were divine covenants; and their place in national history was part of an algorithm encoded before my birth to sculpt my reflection in the mirror. My political allegiances, my feelings of communal love and hatred, and the targets of each were mapped on a road that took me from the delivery ward to the cemetery on the top of that hill, trod by mourning families' seasonal step from what seemed to be time immemorial, onwards to eternity.

This is not to say that I longed for a selfless white hand to dissolve my black veil and expose my face to the sun. I cannot (and I do not wish to) claim the crown of victimhood, at least not in the *Arabian Nights* sense of the term. The domestic space that my family inhabited in Lebanon was a greenhouse of Russianness, for better or for worse—religion was not a welcome guest at the table, and I rarely felt that I was worth less because I was a girl. Still, the smell of boiled cabbage mixed with the interminable stench of Soviet military heroism nauseated me. I belonged in the world outside the looking glass of our closed shutters. But the crush of the mill stone under the sun was far too strong, and I felt that if I stayed in the open air for too long, I risked asphyxiation, like air dried porcelain. And I—I wanted something else: to be eternally versatile clay bent to my own fingers' caprice. A sheet of glass that refrains from absorbing the rain, no matter how forcefully the rain pounds its surface.

But the rain turned into a waterfall, and the glass cracked. When the July 2006 War fell upon us with its sleet of rockets, they dropped right onto my heirlooms of trauma, my dowry into the house of life. As a child of the so-called Lebanese post-war generation, I was never old enough to consciously remember the fifteen-year civil war that cracked the nation apart like a ripe pomegranate. Many of the war's survivors (it seemed to me) live on a diet of bitterness and PTSD tucked under the glossy cover of collective amnesia. But the war stormed in, and my instincts somehow picked up the geographical range of falling bombs; I knew when to tape the windows to prevent their shattered bits from nailing me to the wall, and knew that the safest places to sleep during a nightly raid were the hallway and the bathtub, in the absence of an underground car garage. Where had I learned these invaluable life skills, I did not know. They were in the water, they were in the air; I absorbed them with pervasive secondhand smoke, and they sedimented in my flesh. To be certain, I had grown up in a war zone. The line between war and peace in Lebanon is weaved by the smoke of guns. The War, however, has a special place in the pantheon of Lebaneseness. Under the bombs, I saw my future before me, reflected in the lusterless eyes of the past's embodied ghosts.

If The War were to rise from the dead and break the backs of my generation, I was not ready to take my place in conflict's chain of reincarnations; I was not prepared to be a sheep to the slaughter, pulled against my will into the cyclical twist of eternal return. I had no reason to sacrifice myself for a string of meaningless metaphors, nation-honor-loyalty, relentlessly reiterated like the dull hum of an engine, numbing minds to the buzz of their meaning.

I understand now that I wrote *Ali* to escape the deep sense of aversion that slid on the walls of my stomach while I constructed the narrator's latent homophobia and her bigotry towards the Russian sex workers. I think that this is exactly how it feels to be imprisoned within a system of power where the emancipation of one's self deceptively necessitates the crushing of others' bones.

I also wrote *Ali* to escape the taint of history. But, unbeknownst to myself, I constructed a character that was wrapped in mappings much larger than himself, not only a victim of History proper, but a culprit of geopolitics and coincidence. I was fascinated by the packages of mass-produced hatred that public consensus incessantly left at my doorstep—the same structures that, much larger than Ali, had made him his own enemy. This contempt seemed to be a rare homogenizing matrix in Lebanon's kaleidoscopic national landscape. It stung even Lebanese liberals, who monotonously chewed on the complicated nature of sectarian identity and shook their warning fingers at the idiocy of religious violence and hatred. By doing so, they meticulously cultivated the circumference of their individualities, painstakingly distancing themselves from the corrupt decisions of their government, the regressive leaders of their sect, the degenerate nature of their religions, and the rot of Lebanese regionalism, but one step outside Lebanon's borders was all it took for hatred to wear a different mask, the mask of mass inclusion. Somehow, magically, the new clothes of contempt became simplicity and pervasiveness. Suddenly, an entire population right outside the nation's borders came to unequivocally represent their government, their religion. There was no complexity "over there," no structures of internal oppression, and no attempt "over here" to understand individuals from "over there"—for what? Above the skies of *that* heart of darkness, one cry had to reign above all: "exterminate the brutes!"

But could Ali really disavow the antagonism within himself with the simple wave of a hand? And how are identities formed if not against *something*?

Like Ali, I was my own enemy, perhaps to a lesser degree. If the legacy of The "civil" War, still fresh in the freezers of Lebanon's memory palace, were to return, it might so happen for me to be shot at a checkpoint—the

101

quintessential symbol of Lebanon's fifteen years of sectarian violence. We, as Lebanese, have to carry our inherited religious, sectarian, and regional identities, Cain-like; they are a conscription that stains us to this day like an unwashable spot, embedded in our legal documents and etched onto our bones. If The War were to return, being of the opposite camp, "belonging" to a religion I do not believe in (and what if I did?) could cost me a bullet in my gut. Exiting the stream of history onto a fixed pedestal of omniscience proved to be a more difficult task than I had ever imagined, and this "objective" vantage point seemed to be fashioned from the shards of one's fragmented flesh.

And then I understood—I *am* the stuff of history. Of course, we all are to a large extent, but in my case the inorganic nature of my conception amplified the facts. My entire existence is inextricably bound to a fleeting historical moment: the tight window of Soviet-Arab educational exchanges. The possibility of a meeting between my parents and people like them stretched over some forty years, and that window was ultimately barred when the hammer hit the sickle.

After the rubble of the Soviet Union rose to the world's eyes, and long after memory ebbed and the world's attention turned towards the Kremlin's current monarchy, the children of that historical moment, of its fortuitous Soviet-Arab unions, remain the living souvenirs of a bygone era. The Russianness that we "belong" to is diaphanous, separated from us not merely by time's filter, but by the mushroomed fracking of post-Soviet national identities. If our past is now a foreign country, have I even been there? As once immigrants celebrate Soviet holidays in today's Lebanese cities, I write about chimeric Russianness in an Arabic not spoken. It is double-edgily painful that my mother cannot read me in my mother tongue, but this is the lot of so many of the world's immigrants.

Right now, I feel a sour tinge of this on my tongue as I write about what I wrote about six years ago, in the glare of the New Haven snow pouring through my window, and in English, a language somewhat anesthetized by the global flows of culture. Five years in the United States have recycled my past into yet another foreign country. Ultimately, rereading *Ali and His Russian Mother* through the dual filter of language and time renders my past self foreign, a dancing image receding in the hot desert sun. But there are moments when, while reading presently, my mind constructs an image, or a metaphor, only to discover that the person who was I six years ago has already turned the phrase onto the very same path—word for word. Somehow, it seems, we unwittingly and incessantly tread our sketched mental paths, our ways of constructing our thoughts, and the manners in which we construct ourselves through language and outside of it.

And I must admit, displacement has started to feel a little bit like home. Only sometimes.

TRANSLATOR'S NOTE

It was in the summer of 2006, on the twelfth of July. I was in Montreal, pregnant, having just postponed a trip to Lebanon. News of the war there flashed across my computer screen, friends started calling from all around the world, everyone wondering what was happening. Then the emails started coming in from other people, colleagues, students, and friends, all people trapped under bombardment—in Beirut and elsewhere—not knowing how or if they could escape. The war that summer targeted and affected thousands. It destroyed Lebanon's infrastructure and created a new generation in Lebanon scarred by its daily realities. That summer, most young people in Lebanon did not really remember the Civil War through their own memories; for the most part it was their parents' (and grandparents') war. The period from 1975-1990 is remembered as history to those who were toddlers, babies, or not even born as it was ending. But after the devastation Israel wrought that summer, especially on South Lebanon and the Southern suburbs of Beirut, these young people now could add their own trauma of living in war to that of their parents, grandparents, family, and friends. Remembering that summer of 2006 was crucial to my process of thinking about how to transform Alexandra Chreiteh's second novel, *Ali wa ummuhu al-russiyah* into what is now *Ali and His Russian Mother*.

Montreal is a world away from Beirut, especially during wartime. Even as electricity would come and go, the Internet and speed of communication made it possible to be in closer touch with people in Lebanon during the summer of 2006 than ever before. Observing from afar, following the news daily, hourly, compulsively and worrying about loved ones living in these conditions is a very different experience than living through it yourself. How people are connected through their simultaneous proximity and distance to each other—and to war and violence—has come into clearer focus through faster and more connected communication as well as ongoing and ever-deepening imperial relations between North America and the Arab world. These connections, built upon simultaneous proximity and distance—between communities and people living in war and their families and loved ones who live far away—are paralleled in *Ali and His Russian Mother* in a number of ways. While working with the editor to make final improvements to this translation, the twinned concepts of distance and proximity kept recurring to me as a way to give the reader some insights into the translation process of *Ali and His Russian Mother*.

Dryly subtle humor like that of *Ali and His Russian Mother* is difficult to convey in translation. This short novel is a devastatingly humorous take on the experiences of one young woman and the people around her when she joins the Russian evacuation of its nationals during the 2006 war. Alexandra Chreiteh employs her signature wit and cynicism to gently poke fun at the more trivial concerns of the Lebanese youth of her generation while at the same time tackling difficult issues like homophobia, anti-Jewish feeling, and society's double standards for men and women. Approaching the translation of a text that is extremely funny in the original Arabic, but focused on serious issues, means that the language I strove to create in English needed a light touch, but one that would be funny.

The Arabic language of *Ali and His Russian Mother* very much echoes that of Chreiteh's debut novel, *Always Coca-Cola*. Unsurprisingly, many of the same concerns informed my translations of both. Both are written in an accessible version of standard formal Arabic and thus strike a formal tone because they deal with everyday topics that people usually talk about in everyday colloquial Lebanese Arabic. *Ali and His Russian Mother* uses this more formal language to register complaints about nagging parents, the pain of urinary tract infections, and a possible tissue shortage in the South, just as *Always Coca-Cola* talks about periods, tampons, abortions. My biggest challenge with these works is how to make the

107

English sound as snappy, concise, and funny as the Arabic is, while still retaining some of the stilted formality of standard Arabic. Chreiteh's slightly skewed sense of humor is ironic and cynical, but also gentle.

To capture this humor means to capture the gently snarky tone of the unnamed female narrator. She shares a similar class background to *Always Coca-Cola*'s Abeer Ward—they both are students at the Lebanese American University in Beirut. Unlike Beiruti Abeer though, this young woman originally hails from the Southern town, Nabatiyyeh, whose conservatism stifles her and—like Ali of the title—she also has a Russian mother. This narrator is a bit more mature than Abeer and she tackles serious topics directly and explicitly, while delivering her social commentary with humorous reflections. As her hometown burns under bombardment by Israel and she worries about a ground invasion, the narrator complains of being hungry and needing to pee. Ali's poignant observations about Jewish identity show anti-Jewish feeling in Lebanon to be real and urgent, but she also chides Ali for being paranoid and childish—while gently poking fun at him for not eating pork. The complications of internalized homophobia, living as a gay man both in Lebanon and as a Lebanese man abroad, are fleshed out with examples that tease Ali while valuing his experiences.

Chreiteh's characteristic humor, biting wit, and keen powers of social observation mark this text in Arabic but do not always easily translate into English. The original work had no breaks in the narration and is presented as one continuous flow of words with very little space between them. The work is not divided into chapters or sections. One strategy in presenting the translation, therefore, was to add breaks in the spacing between some paragraphs and sections to improve the reading experience in English. Our decision to change this format was meant not only to make the reading of the translation "easier" but also to create more spaces and pauses for humor and irony to be absorbed and even to punctuate certain moments. This was not needed in the original text where the language alone achieves this effect.

Another way that I thought about capturing the narrative voice of this translation was the balance between how many words should be left in transliterated Arabic and how many translated into a more "domesticated" or smoothly-reading English. *Ali and His Russian Mother* did not provide many obvious opportunities to incorporate untranslated Arabic words. This made decisions about how to deal with individual words both easier and more difficult. When there are fewer words left in Arabic, they stand out more. One such example is the title of Lebanese national icon Fairouz's famous anthem to the city of Jerusalem, "Zahrat al-Madaen" ("Flower of Cities"). Including only the English title led me to wonder whether or not it would resonate at all with readers of the translation who did not know Arabic, or if it would just be a title without meaning. I knew that the title in Arabic, "Zahrat al-Madaen," would immediately conjure up the song—and the image of the city itself and the Palestinian struggle—to readers who do know Arabic. Readers who are more comfortable reading novels in English but know Arabic music and culture will also identify this. In the end, I decided that the benefits of using the Arabic title "Zahrat al-Madaen" with a translation afterward outweighed the possible benefits of translating it directly into English. I used the spelling found on YouTube videos of the song, hoping that people might Google it (and maybe even use the song as a soundtrack for their reading of the novel!).

Food is as central to the translation and transmission of culture as language and music. It is no surprise then that another difficult translation choice was how to render an expression involving kefta. In the novel, Ali's mother threatens a Syrian official who whispers a rude insinuation to her by saying she will make him into kefta—a mixture of ground meat, vegetable, and spices that must be vigorously mashed together. Ali's blonde, "Russian" (Ukrainian) mother who speaks fluent Arabic telling off a Syrian government employee in this way is hilarious in the original text. Would a reader who only knows English recognize this image? I considered and debated different options: leaving the expression and risk making it overly "exotic" if the reader did not know the food; changing it to something more obvious in English like "meatball;" or finding a new expression that gave an equivalent meaning. Because "making someone into a meatball" conjured up an entirely different sort of beating than the one I visualized with a woman mashing up her kefta in the kitchen, I opted for the latter. In the end, I settled on making it slightly more idiomatic in English while retaining some of its local flavor, and capturing the humorous implied violence differently, "She slapped him hard and ordered him to get away from her—if not, she'd skewer him like a kabab!" (p. 85).

Another technique that is difficult to convey in English is the use of repetition and exaggeration; the narrator's sense of urgency about mundane issues is part of the authorial strategy to satirize her generation. Capturing this voice in translation is less difficult than making it sound funny in English. Part of the effect of exaggeration is achieved by using the formal Arabic language in place of the spoken language in which the events would have taken place. The constant complaining about needing to pee is one example. This is almost impossible to reproduce, though in places the stilted English is meant to approximate Chreiteh's play with linguistic registers—in this case her "taking care of her needs."

The final example here that I spent a long time experimenting with is how Ali consciously and humorously uses expressions that mimic how old women talk. The way in which he interjects such expressions into his speech has immediately recognizable gendered and generational connotations. This use of "women's language" by a man struggling with his gender and sexuality is central to the text and impossible to reproduce exactly in translation. One phrase he uses in Arabic, for example, is "*tistritk sitr,*" an interjection full of meaning, but which has no translation. It punctuates what has already been said and easily understood in context. In one case, I tried to convey the sense of expression, by translating it "Oooh, odd choice" (p. 26). Here Ali is reacting to the narrator's decision to study filmmaking. "Oooh" is meant to convey the interjectional nature of the expression. To balance this, I then also leave in Arabic the narrator's ironic response where she calls him "hajjeh"—a respectful title for an older woman. I was careful to emphasize the cushioning expressions that give these phrases more meaning like how he "strikes his cheeks," or speaks "like women" or "like the old women in Nabatiyyeh."

All of the examples of translating humorous expressions above speak to the possibilities and limitations of translation. Like translation, humor brings people together—we use humor to connect to each other, we laugh together at jokes, we look in someone's eyes when we experience something funny. But humor is profoundly alienating when you don't "get it." The work of the translator is to help you "get it" while preserving the elements that make it funny in the first place—without too much explanation. Thinking about humor through the lens of distance and proximity to a text is another way to reflect on the process of translation. The experience of living in Lebanon in 2006 during the war "there" is profoundly different than living in Montreal, or wherever else is "not there." Finding ways to come closer to the text—feeling, understanding, and conveying its experiences—is about the negotiation between here and there, as much as it is about English and Arabic. This is one thing that makes *Ali and His Russian Mother* so interesting to read and think about in translation.

Michelle Hartman

Translator's Acknowledgments

My first and most heartfelt thanks to Alexandra Chreiteh for entrusting me with another novel and for being so open to conversation about this translation, other literary works, and questions of language and translation. The team at Interlink, Michel Moushabeck and everyone else, was always supportive and continue to tirelessly promote the translation of Arabic fiction. This includes the wonderful editor John Fiscella, who deserves much credit for the final shape of the translation and for pushing me to think deeply about many ways to improve it. Bader Takriti, Katy Kalemkerian, Ralph Haddad, and Aziz Choudry provided invaluable help and support. Merci kteer, I am lucky to have been able to work with all of you. Thanks to Tameem for patience when you had it. This is the first translation that you helped me with—while delayed in an airport—perhaps it's a sign of things to come.

This translation is dedicated to all those who don't quite fit where they are, in Lebanon and elsewhere... queer, Muslim, Jewish, Black, and especially all those "in-between."